860-768-0201
Mom
work
Sue
13
Rye St. Park
45 Dower
Blue ranch
11:30 A.M.

To Sean Georgiades:

Best wishes!

Splat!

Andre J. Garant

authorHOUSE

AuthorHouse™
1663 Liberty Drive
Bloomington, IN 47403
www.authorhouse.com
Phone: 1-800-839-8640

© 2011 Andre J. Garant. All rights reserved.

No part of this book may be reproduced, stored in a retrieval system, or transmitted by any means without the written permission of the author.

First published by AuthorHouse 1/17/2011

ISBN: 978-1-4567-2152-7 (sc)
ISBN: 978-1-4567-2151-0 (e)

Printed in the United States of America

Any people depicted in stock imagery provided by Thinkstock are models,
and such images are being used for illustrative purposes only.
Certain stock imagery © Thinkstock.

This book is printed on acid-free paper.

Because of the dynamic nature of the Internet, any Web addresses or links contained in this book may have changed since publication and may no longer be valid. The views expressed in this work are solely those of the author and do not necessarily reflect the views of the publisher, and the publisher hereby disclaims any responsibility for them.

DEDICATION

This story is dedicated to all of the wonderful fourth graders at Eli Terry School in South Windsor, Connecticut. I first met this fantastic bunch of kids during a writing workshop in January, 2010 and knew right away that they would be so much fun to write about. So, before reading this book, it might be nice to introduce all of these boys and girls by first name. The superstars who had Mrs. Crook last year are London, Griffin, Maxim, Sean, Alexander, Maria, Cassidy, Christopher, Garrett, Zola, Andrew, William, Brandon, Jack, Jacob, Madison, Dakota, James, Jenny, Jonathan, and Sydney.

The hotshots in Mrs. Desmarais's class last year are Hannah, Zachary, Aaron, Stefan, Sean, Grace, Brianna, Eric, Ethan, Melody, Connor, Camille, Anthony, Camryn, Donald, Jason, Summer, Ainsley, Geena, Justin, and Matthew. The celebrities in Mrs. Shelley's class last year are Ryan, Meghan, Erin, Jared, Sierra, Brianna, Adrian, Noah, Ashley, Joey (the main character!), Sean, Christopher, Jacob, Alexandra, Amanda, John, Stephon, Jacob, and last but certainly not least, another Jacob!

These incredible boys and girls have an amazing sense of adventure and humor that lends itself nicely to any book. When I announced to them in May, 2010 that they would be characters in my new book, they were thrilled beyond belief.

Andre J. Garant

I couldn't have chosen a more wonderful bunch of students to feature in one of my stories. I hope that this book will always serve to remind these kids just how special they are, not only to their parents and teachers, but also to me. I will always remember each one of you with fond memories of our exciting project at Eli Terry School. Always reach for the stars and be the very best you can be in life!

LAST NAMES & NICKNAMES

To keep <u>Splat!</u> as simple as possible, I decided against using any last names. However, in certain cases, it was necessary to refer to a student as 'Jacob M.' since there are four boys named Jacob and three boys named Sean. Wow! Therefore, all students will be referred to by their first name only unless there are more than one student with the same name. Also, even though many of the kids in the story provided nicknames that they preferred to be called by, I have decided to keep them to a minimum in the story. However, there are certain kids whose nicknames actually worked well in the story, and so those students who are referred to by nicknames are as follows.

Alexandra will be 'Alex', Amanda will be 'Mandy', Andrew will be 'Andy', Christopher L. will be 'CJ', Jacob Slahtosky will be 'Jake', Matthew will be 'Matt', Maxim will be 'Max', Meghan will be 'Meg', William will be 'Billy', and Zachary will be 'Zach'. All other students are referred to by their <u>real</u> first name. And so there you have it, the rundown on last names & nicknames in the story. If you are able to read this story without getting totally confused, then you must be a genius! Can you imagine being the author and trying to keep all of these names straight while writing the book? Golly Gee!

Contents

DEDICATION v
LAST NAMES & NICKNAMES vii
JOEY'S AMAZING OPPORTUNITY 1
THE BIG MOMENT 9
1966 GALORE! 17
HOT DOG HEAVEN 27
JAKE TAKES THE CAKE................................. 37
WE'RE ALL WINNERS! 49
SPLAT!... 63
ELI TERRY JEOPARDY 73
THE OLDEN DAYS.. 85

JOEY'S AMAZING OPPORTUNITY

"Joey, come on, it's time to get up for school," Mom hollered to me from down the hall. "I can't be late for work again today, honey."

"What?" I mumbled in a groggy voice, wishing I could just stick my head back under the covers and fall asleep once again.

In less time than you could sneeze, Mom busted into my bedroom and raised the blinds on my window. "Come on, sweetie, you can sleep in on Saturday. It's time for school."

"Aw, ma," I muttered, my eyes half open now. "What's so important about school, anyway?"

"Don't get me started today, Joseph," my mother responded, using my full name to warn me that I had better get moving and cut out the nonsense.

"Hey," I shouted as my mother pulled the comforter right off my bed, now leaving me in my spongebob pajamas that were starting to get a little too small on me.

Mom then reached down and planted a kiss on my forehead before ruffling my mop of shaggy, brown hair that was badly in need of being cut. "Breakfast is already on the table and I picked out your clothes, Joey. You have a nice pair of denim shorts and your favorite orange dragon shirt."

I sat up in bed and squinted my eyes from the

bright sunlight streaming in the window. "Geez, Mom, I can pick out my own clothes now, don't you think? I mean, I'm going to be ten years old next month."

"Oh, sweetie, don't remind me of your birthday. You're growing up way too fast for me."

I sneered. "Yeah, right." Before I could say anything else, my mother was already out the door in a flash and flying down the stairs, always a perpetual whirlwind of energy in the morning. I was the complete opposite; slow and lazy. Once I got to school, I was fine, however, it was just the mornings that I didn't like.

By the time I arrived at school, I wondered what might make today such an exciting day like our fourth grade teachers had promised us all week. I mean, what could possibly be so amazing about digging up a time capsule from 1966? My teacher, Mr. Federici, kept saying over and over how great it would be to learn some things from back when he was a kid our age, but if we had the choice about going to Six Flags or digging up a time capsule, it was no contest whatsoever. Well, actually, if staying here at Eli Terry meant that I wouldn't have to sit next to Jonathan all day long on the rides as he pretended to throw up on me, then digging up the time capsule might not be all that bad after all.

"Good morning, Joey," Mr. Federici said to me as I strolled into the classroom and took my seat in the front row.

"What's so great about it?"

"Joey, that's not very nice," my teacher said with a smile. He then walked up to me. "Is everything okay with you today?"

Splat!

I shrugged my shoulders. "I guess so. I'm just kind of bummed out that we're not going to Six Flags like the fifth graders this year."

Mr. Federici chuckled at me. "Oh, is that what's got you down a little? Well, I think you can put on your happy face today since we're going to have a boatload of fun digging up the time capsule in a little bit."

I flashed my teacher the biggest smile I could muster up, even if it was a bit fake. "Okay, I'll try to be happy."

"Attaboy," Mr. Federici said with a pat on my back. "Now there's the Joey I know so well."

"Dude, this time capsule thing is gonna rock," Aaron muttered from the seat behind me. "I hope we find some dinosaur bones in there."

"From 1966?" Summer questioned. "I doubt it, Aaron. It's not like my father was born when dinosaurs were still around."

"My father's older than forty-five years old," Ryan remarked. "He's forty-six."

"I wonder if they had cars back then," Justin inquired while scratching his chin.

"Or telephones," Genna asked. "My grandmother was born right after World War Two, so I don't think they even had telephones back then."

Mr. Federici overheard us as he came walking back up the aisle. "Like I said, kids, there is a lot of exciting stuff to learn about with the time capsule being dug up."

"When were you born, Mr. Federici?" Cassidy asked our teacher.

"Um, let's just say it was after 1966, but that's not for you to know."

"Yeah, Cassidy, remember last year when we

Andre J. Garant

learned that some questions are personal and you just don't ask them?" Andy stated. "It's like asking your mother what size waist she has."

"Or, better yet, what size underwear your Aunt Edna has on," Eric blurted out before we all busted out laughing.

"Oh, Eric, we can always count on you for a good laugh," Mr. Federici said with a smile. "I'm certainly going to miss you when you move up to fifth grade next year."

"If you guys want some good jokes, I have quite a few to share," Brandon informed us.

Mr. Federici held up his hand to halt Brandon from going to town. "That's okay, Brandon, we're about to start class right now."

"Aww, darn it," I muttered, always one to appreciate a good joke.

Just then, our principal, Mrs. Sevick, came over the intercom. "Good morning, boys and girls at Eli Terry School. Today we have a very special event planned for all of our students." Mrs. Sevick hesitated for a few seconds, causing lots of oohs and aahs to sound throughout the classroom. "At eleven o'clock, we are going to be gathering in the courtyard so we can dig up the time capsule that was buried here back in May of 1966. Today marks the forty-fifth anniversary of the time capsule and is when it is supposed to be dug up." At once, a huge round of applause sounded throughout the entire school, resonating up each and every corridor. "One of our fourth grade classrooms, that of Mr. Federici, will be leading the opening process of the time capsule and taking out the items one by one so that we can all learn what was important back in 1966."

Splat!

"Can I do that, Mr. Fedrici?" Jake hollered, his voice nearly shattering the classroom windows. "I think it would be a great job for me."

"Just a second, class, the principal is not finished yet," Mr. Federici said, wanting us all to quiet down.

We all squirmed in our seats as we waited for Mrs. Sevick to end the morning announcements, and when it came to stand up and pledge allegiance to the flag, I began to get excited that my class had been chosen to open up the time capsule. Mr. Federici had already informed us yesterday that one of the fourth grade classrooms would be given the honors after we had scored best on the CMT exams.

"Okay, kids, who wants to open up the time capsule?" Mr. Federici asked us before an explosion of screaming and yelling sounded throughout the classroom.

I nearly tripped over my own two feet as I pushed and shoved with the other kids to scramble to the front of the classroom, my hand raised high over my head. Being one of the tallest kids in the fourth grade certainly gave me an advantage in making myself known.

Mr. Federici glanced in my direction and nodded his head at me. "Joey, we'll start with you today, but to be fair, we'll alternate so that all of the kids have a chance to take something out of the time capsule."

"Yes," I shouted in my loudest voice as I pumped my fist in the air twice. "I rock, dudes."

"Aww, man, how come Joey gets to go first?" Maria asked. "Why can't a girl be picked to go first?"

Andre J. Garant

"Quiet down, everyone," Mr. Federici announced, doing his best to calm down a bunch of overly excited fourth graders, but it was no use. In fact, many of the boys were jumping around so crazily that it appeared they all had ants down their pants. "We'll start off with Joey and then the rest of you can have a chance. Just remember to do a good job today since the rest of the school will be watching you."

"Thank you, Mr. Federici," I said, my entire face now beaming from ear to ear at being picked to go first. Maybe not going to Six Flags wasn't all that bad after all.

A few minutes later, Mrs. Sevick poked her head in our classroom door. "Congratulations, kids. And just who is the lucky student who got picked to open up the capsule door?"

On cue, all of my classmates called out my name and pointed their fingers in my direction.

Mrs. Sevick then walked up to me with a grin on her face. "Wow, Joey, that's quite an honor for a nice boy like you. Are you excited about this opportunity?"

"Yup, for sure," I said while nodding my head a few times. "I can't wait."

Our principal playfully pinched my cheek. "Wow, I can't remember ever seeing you so excited about anything before. This is wonderful."

"Do we get to keep any of the stuff we take out of the time capsule, Mrs. Sevick?" Jenny asked.

"Yeah, if there's like a real famous baseball in there, can I take it home?" Connor asked.

Mrs. Sevick shrugged her shoulders. "Well, there were no instructions written down from the teacher who buried it, but I'm not sure that's a good idea. I think we might put everything back inside and re-bury the time capsule for another class at some point in the future."

"Did they have TV's and computers back in 1966?" Anthony asked. "I think my aunt Sally is forty-five years old."

"Well, they definitely had televisions, but I'm not sure about computers," Mrs. Sevick answered. "But, what TV's they had were black and white for the most part and they didn't have these big fancy, flat screens like we have nowadays."

"My uncle told me he was going to buy a Mustang from 1966, but he didn't have the money at the time and somebody else bought it," Jack stated matter-of-factly.

Mrs. Sevick smiled. "Oh, the Ford Mustang was a very popular car back in those days. In fact, my first boyfriend had an old one that his father gave him. I think it was a 1965 and it had superb vinyl seats." Our principal's eyes glazed over as she glanced at the far wall with a big smile on her face.

"But, Mrs. Sevick, you're not that old, are you?" I asked, quickly snapping her out of her own daydream.

"That's right, Joey, I'm only twenty-six years old," our principal stated with mock authority while quickly ruffling my hair. "Okay, kids, we'll see you outside in a little while."

After our principal left, Eric turned to face me. "Is she really that young?"

I laughed out loud. "I have no idea, Eric. Let's pay attention to what she says later on when we open the time capsule."

And so there it was, the start of a very cool day for me, Joey Hence, a typical fourth-grade boy at Eli Terry School.

THE BIG MOMENT

At 11:00, the entire student body of Eli Terry School filed outside into the courtyard. It was quite a scene getting that many kids into one space all at once, but we managed to do it. Seeing as our class had the honors of opening up the time capsule, we were right up in the front near the hole where the time capsule had been buried.

Mrs. Sevick turned on the microphone. "Good morning, boys and girls." At once, everyone began to quiet down. "At last, the moment we have been waiting for all morning has arrived. It's now time to open up our time capsule." With that said, everyone began cheering and clapping. "This is a very special day for our school as we open up a time capsule from 1966."

Just then, Brianna D. raised her hand. "Mrs. Sevick, why are we digging up the time capsule this year and not waiting until it's fifty years old?"

Mr. Federici glanced at Brianna and nodded his head. "Great question."

Mrs. Sevick agreed at once. "Yes, that is a wonderful question to ask, so let me answer it. The reason why we are digging up the time capsule now and not waiting another five years is that the instructions that were left behind said we should open up the capsule anytime after the year 2000. Also, since our school won the Blue Ribbon Award

Andre J. Garant

ten years ago, we felt that this was the perfect time to celebrate such a wonderful occasion."

CJ shrugged his shoulders as he stood next to me. "Ah, forty-five years or fifty years; same difference."

Donny nodded his head. "Yeah, not much will change in five years from now."

Hannah begged to differ. "I wouldn't be so sure about that, Donny. After all, in five years from now, we might have talking cars."

"We already do have talking cars, silly," Jimmy argued. "My father's car has a GPS system that talks to him all the way to work."

"Yeah, but I'll bet in five years cars will be able to make you coffee and even change baby diapers in the back seat," Jonathan stated with a tone of authority.

"Only you would say something as silly as that, Jonathan," Ainsley commented while pasting her hands to her hips.

"Okay, everyone, let's stop talking and pay attention to what's going on," Mr. Federici insisted, giving us the evil eye that signaled for all chit chat to stop at once.

Mrs. Sevick then glanced in my direction. "Joey, are you ready to begin the celebration this morning?"

I nodded my head with eagerness. "Yup, just tell me what to do."

Our principal then walked over to me with the microphone in her hand. "Joey Hence will be our student this morning who has the honors of opening up the time capsule. He will then take out the first item that was buried back in 1966." The crowd of kids around me began to get very

Splat!

excited as I walked up to the giant hole where the time capsule lay, now surrounded by piles of fresh dirt that had been dug up earlier this morning by the school janitors. "Joey, the latch to open the time capsule is right there on the side, so why don't you open it up."

"Okay," I muttered as I glanced around and felt the latch with my fingers. I lifted up on the handle and pulled open the door. At once, the crowd of kids and teachers surrounding me began to clap. The door to the capsule opened up on its own as everyone began glancing at all of the items placed inside. They sure did look old to me!

"Joey will now take out one item and we will discuss them one by one," Mrs. Sevick announced to the group. "Then, we will divide up the items so that each classroom can take a few things back and talk about them. By the time Friday rolls around, each of you will know more about what life was like back in 1966."

"Are we going to have a test on this stuff?" Alexander asked with a frown on his face.

"Yeah, do we have to actually pay attention today?" Garrett asked.

Mrs. Sevick nodded her head. "Well, actually, I wasn't planning on giving any tests, but I do think a nice oral or written report will be a good idea so that we can all learn from this experience."

"Aw, man, are you kidding me now?" Matthew hollered. At once, Mrs. Bowden told him to quiet down.

"Joey, what item would you like to take out of the capsule right now?" Mrs. Sevick asked me, now turning her attention back to the ceremony.

I glanced down into the time capsule and saw

Andre J. Garant

a small brochure on Eli Terry School. I picked it up with my hands and held it up in the air for everyone to see. "It says something about Eli Terry being the first all-electric school in Connecticut."

"Wow, that is very interesting, Joey," Mrs. Sevick remarked as she reached to take the brochure out of my hands. "I was aware of this, but I never saw the actual brochure that described what made Eli Terry an all-electric school."

"What does it say?" Melody asked. "Can you read it to us?"

Mrs. Sevick placed her reading glasses on the edge of her nose and began to read a few passages from the brochure. "Actual construction began on August 1, 1964 and the new school opened its doors to students on September 20, 1965. Eli Terry Elementary School dramatically illustrates electric heat's money-saving versatility."

"We have electric heat in our house, too," Stephon announced. "My father says it's more expensive than oil heat, but it's much cleaner."

"We also have electric heat in our house," Zola pointed out. "It's only bad when we lose power and then have no heat."

"Boys and girls, this is a fascinating school that we all attend since it was one of the first in the United States to have all-electric heat," Mrs. Sevick called out. "Back in 1965, that was a huge milestone in engineering since nearly all schools were heated with oil that was very dirty and costly."

"What else is in the capsule, Joey?" Grace asked me. "Pick out something else that we can learn about."

Splat!

I reached into the time capsule and picked up a large flat picture that said *Herb Alpert: A Taste Of Honey* on it.

"Wow, it's a record from 1966," Mrs. Bowden called out. "Herb Alpert was a famous jazz musician back then."

"Holy cow, my father has a huge collection of records just like that in our basement," Mandy cried out. "He's always playing them on an old record player with a needle."

"Boys and girls, that is how people listened to music back in 1966," Mrs. Sevick remarked. "There were no such things as CD's, Ipod's, MP3 players, and all of that jazz we have today."

"Yeah, and the records used to skip all the time, too, when the needle got worn out and needed to be replaced," Camille told us.

"How do you know about that?" Ethan asked his classmate.

Camille merely shrugged her shoulders. "Because my grandmother told me all about it."

"Pick another item, Joey," Adrian called out. "This is really fun."

"I had a feeling you guys would like the time capsule," Mr. Federici stated. "It's a lot of fun for me, too, seeing as I'm too young to know what life was like back then."

"Just how old are you, Mr. Federici?" Dakota inquired of her teacher.

Mr. Federici merely smiled at us. "Some secrets are worth keeping."

Griffin chuckled. "Besides, don't you know it's rude to ask an adult how old they are, Dakota?"

"Yeah, my grandmother tells me that all the

Andre J. Garant

time," Jacob L. remarked. "I guess I asked her the question a few too many times."

"Okay, Joey, pick out another item, please," Mrs. Sevick called out, turning my attention back to the time capsule. "We have a lot of stuff to do today just yet."

"What else are we doing today besides the time capsule?" Jared asked our principal.

"It's a secret," Mrs. Sevick stated while pinching the boy's cheek, causing him to giggle.

I gasped when I unfolded the grey tee shirt in my hands that had *Baltimore Orioles* written across the front. Attached to the shirt was a piece of paper held by a safety pin. "Wow, check this out."

"Read it to us, Joey," Mrs. Bowden insisted.

I unfolded the piece of paper in my hands. "This year, the Baltimore Orioles defeated the Los Angeles Dodgers in the baseball World Series by a score of four to nothing. This tee shirt was purchased in Baltimore by a teacher of Eli Terry School on a trip there about three weeks after the World Series game."

"Awesome, can I keep that shirt?" London cried out. "I love the Orioles. They have some super cool players on their team."

"Unfortunately, London, nobody can take any of the items from the time capsule," Mrs. Sevick declared. "Everything needs to go back inside after we have used them for discussion purposes in the classroom."

"Can I wear it home one day, then?" London asked, not giving in so easily. "It looks like the perfect size for a fourth grader."

"Tell you what, London, we'll let you try it on

Splat!

sometime this week," Mrs. Bowden called out, knowing exactly what to say to make the boy smile with glee.

I tossed the tee shirt over to London. "Here, you can hold onto it for a while."

"Let's have someone else take a few things out of the time capsule now," Mrs. Sevick announced. "Thank you so much, Joey, for doing a wonderful job today." Everyone gave me a round of applause as I bowed my head to the crowd.

Mr. Federici gave me a big pat on the back as I walked over to him. "So, how was your big moment of fame, Joey?"

I gave off a huge smile. "It was pretty cool."

"The fun is just beginning," my teacher stated. "We have some really fun things planned for you guys today. Let's just say it's a kind of fourth grade recognition day."

"I think fourth grade has been the best year of my life so far," I said proudly. "I wish it wasn't ending so soon."

Mr. Federici seemed surprised. "You mean you don't want to move up to fifth grade next year?"

"Hey, I didn't say that," I blurted out. "I just don't want this year to end so soon. I'm really going to miss everyone over the summer."

Mr. Federici smiled widely. "Yeah, I'll miss you guys, too, but we still have a few weeks left, so let's not get depressed so soon, okay?"

I nodded my head. "Yeah, okay."

1966 GALORE!

"Billy, why don't you come up and take something out of the time capsule now," Mrs. Sevick announced, pointing to my classmate standing right in back of me.

"Oh, boy, this is very exciting," Billy mentioned as he stepped up and grabbed onto a piece of paper that was folded in half. "Let's see what this says." After unfolding the paper, he noticed that it had prices of what things cost back in 1966 and then held it up for Mrs. Sevick to see.

"Read it out loud to us, sweetie," our principal suggested.

"This is a list of what some things cost today in 1966. For example, a package of bacon is only seventy-two cents a pound, eggs are only thirty-six cents per dozen, and a loaf of freshly baked bread is only twenty-two cents."

"Wow, that sounds real cheap to me," Meg stated. "Can I read some now?" Billy handed the piece of paper to Meg as she continued to read some of the prices back in 1966. "Fresh ground hamburger is forty-five cents per pound, a gallon of milk is one dollar and eleven cents, and ground coffee is only ninety cents per pound."

"That's very impressive," Mrs. Buyak declared. "Does anyone know how much a gallon of milk costs today?"

"Great question," Mrs. Sevick called out.

Andre J. Garant

Max immediately raised his hand. "Um, if I'm right, it's about three dollars and fifty cents."

"Excellent, Max," Mrs. Buyak stated with a smile. "Some places are a bit cheaper than that, but I think that's right on the money."

"What about gas for cars?" Noah asked. "I'm wondering if it says what the price of that is on that piece of paper."

Since we were now taking turns reading from the price sheet, Sydney grabbed it from Meg and scanned the piece of paper. "Here it is. A gallon of gas cost thirty-two cents back in 1966."

"Holy cow," Zach blurted out. "That's like three dollars less than what it costs now."

"Yeah, and it's no wonder why they had big gas guzzlers back then," Stefan admitted. "My uncle still drives a big Cadillac and he says it only gets about ten miles to the gallon."

Sean H. now took the price sheet and looked up the price of a new car. "Wow, a new car back then only cost about two thousand, six hundred dollars."

Jake let out a whistle between his two front teeth. "Holy moses, that's a lot cheaper than the Corvette my Uncle Dave just bought. He told me it was almost seventy thousand dollars for that car, but it's worth every penny."

"Dude, that thing must hum on the highway," Christopher stated with a dreamy look on his face.

"Yeah, and he can chirp the tires so loud that smoke comes out," Jake said. "When I turn eighteen, he said I can drive it, too."

"Only eight more years to go," Jason announced. "Then we'll both be fighting for it."

Splat!

"And while you guys are fighting for it, I'll just sweet talk Uncle Dave for the keys and smoke you both out," Jimmy insisted.

"You guys are just too funny," Mrs. Bowden remarked. "I never thought I'd see the day when I taught identical triplets. I love every minute of it."

"Yeah, so did our babysitter when we were six months old," Jason stated. "She never knew which one of us was pooping like crazy." Everyone busted out laughing from that.

Mrs. Sevick shook her head, although she was smiling at the same time. "Boys, we'd all love to hear about your diaper days, but let's get back to the time capsule. We only have twenty more minutes to this class."

Erin now had the price sheet and looked up the price of a new house. "Wow, everyone, a brand new house only cost fourteen thousand dollars back in 1966."

"That's real cheap," John admitted. "It's hard to buy a car for that price today."

"I've got an interesting question for the price sheet," Mrs. Buyak stated. "Does it say what the average salary for a worker is?"

Erin glanced at the sheet. "It says right here that the average income was six thousand, nine hundred dollars per year."

A lot of oohing and aahing sounded from the fourth graders. "Everyone, let's work on our math skills right now," Mrs. Sevick called out through the microphone. "If a worker makes six thousand, nine hundred dollars per year, then how much is that per month?"

Immediately, Camryn's hand shot up in the

Andre J. Garant

air. "I want to say it's just under six hundred dollars per month."

"Excellent, Camryn," Mrs. Sevick stated. "Now, let's take it one step further and figure out what it was per week."

Brianna H. raised her hand this time. "I think it's around one hundred and fifty dollars."

"Excellent job, everyone," Mr. Federici called out. "I can see that you have been learning quite a bit this year in the classroom."

"I love math," Ashley stated. "It's by far my favorite subject."

Sean D. immediately objected. "Yuk, I hate math. Give me gym and I'm good to go."

"Nah, I'd rather have recess all day long since then you can do whatever you want and don't have to listen to the teacher," Jacob W. stated.

"Okay, let's stay focused now," Mrs. Bowden insisted. "How about a few more items from the price sheet."

Jacob S. grabbed the sheet from Erin. "Okay, I've got a good one. It says here that a postage stamp only cost five cents."

"Wow, that's cheap. They cost forty four cents now," Alex mentioned. "That's quite a bit more."

"Kids, that is what we call inflation. It's the term used to talk about how the prices of certain things increase over time," Mrs. Buyak explained to us.

"Does anyone know what the percentage increase on the postage stamp is?" Mr. Federici asked us.

Madison was quick to do the numbers in her head. "Yup, I know. The cost has increased about

Splat!

nine times, so it would be a nine hundred percent increase."

Mrs. Sevick was genuinely impressed. "Wow, Madison, that was amazing. And you are absolutely correct, too."

"When did you get to be such a genius, Madison?" Sean G. asked his classmate.

Without waiting for an answer, Jacob S. read another item off the price sheet. "How about the cost of a movie ticket? It says here that it cost just over a dollar in 1966."

Sierra's eyes opened wide. "Wow, today you can't go to see a movie for less than seven or eight dollars, depending on what theater you go to."

"And then the silly popcorn costs at least that much," Aaron remarked. "I can usually eat one of the large buckets all by myself."

"Yeah, and then it's fun to lick all the butter off your fingers, too," Brandon stated with a smile.

"Oh, Lord, only with fourth graders," Mrs. Bowden called out.

"You mean you don't lick the butter off your fingers after you eat popcorn, Mrs. Bowden?" Jack asked.

Our fourth grade teacher shook her head. "Nah, not really, boys, although my own kids do that for sure."

"Okay, is that it for prices on the sheet?" Mrs. Sevick asked Jacob S., whereupon the boy nodded his head. "Let's have another student come up and take something else out. We only have a little time left."

Ryan then walked up and grabbed what appeared to be a tube of toothpaste out of the time capsule. He held it up over his head for everyone to see. It was a white tube with the words *Super Stripe* written on the side. "It's toothpaste, everyone."

"Open it up and put some on your teeth, Ryan," Justin cried out.

"Yeah, check around in there and see if there's a toothbrush to use with it," Geena insisted.

Ryan then searched around inside the time capsule but didn't find any toothbrushes. "Darn, I don't see one in here, so I'll just take off the cap and see if this stuff is still good." With that said, the boy unscrewed the cap and squirted some of the white toothpaste onto his finger.

"Are you going to put that in your mouth?" Jenny asked Ryan.

Ryan nodded his head with eagerness. "Sure, why not." He then plopped a small blob of the toothpaste on his tongue and began to taste it. The look of uncertainty on his face made for a great photograph, and Mrs. Buyak snapped one with her digital camera. "Yup, it's toothpaste and it tastes kind of minty."

"That's gross," Summer shouted. "That stuff has been in there for forty five years and you just put some in your mouth, Ryan. How do you know it doesn't have all sorts of germs in it?"

"Or tons of cooties?" Connor hollered, causing everyone to burst out laughing.

Ryan stuck out his tongue to show us the pasty, white substance. "Nope, no cooties. I'm still alive."

Mrs. Sevick merely laughed. "Dear Lord, what else is in there? Someone else come up and take something out."

Anthony jumped at the opportunity and took

Splat!

out a glass jar of some orange stuff. The label on the side was starting to peel off, but we could read the big letters. It appeared to say *Tang*.

"Oh, my goodness, boys and girls," Mrs. Buyak exclaimed. "That drink was very popular right around the time I was born. It was an orange drink that you made from a powder. Everyone claimed the astronauts made it since they used to drink it when they took trips on the space shuttle."

"Open it up, Anthony," Andrew hollered. "Let's taste it."

Anthony struggled to unscrew the cap, but finally got it off and grimaced when he saw the orange powder inside. He stuck his nose into the jar and took a deep whiff. "Yuck, it smells real strong of something orange."

"I love orange stuff," Cassidy stated. "Let me sniff it."

"Okay, everyone, let's not go crazy with the Tang," Mrs. Sevick announced. "I know some of you might want to drink it, but it's probably not safe after all these years."

"Why not?" I cried out. "The cover was on very tight."

"Just the same, Joey, it might have some mold growing in it."

"Oh, that's just sick," Eric declared. "Let's drink that stuff and see if mold grows in our stomach later on."

Maria was not impressed with that idea. "Eric, that is just disgusting. If you boys want to do that, then go right ahead, but us girls are much smarter."

"And while we're at it, let's put the toothpaste

Andre J. Garant

back," Mrs. Bowden announced. "Nobody else should be putting any of that in their mouth. Ryan, perhaps you should go to the water fountain and rinse your mouth out."

"Okay, everyone, we only have time for one more object, so why doesn't Ainsley do us the honors," Mrs. Sevick called out.

Ainsley then walked up to the time capsule and picked out a small cereal box that had *Product 19* written across the front. It looked like some sort of corn flakes to me. "It's a box of cereal from 1966. I've never heard of it."

"Holy cow, who would eat something that's called Product 19?" Griffin hollered. "I only eat stuff like Boo Berry and Count Chocula."

"I wonder if they ever made a Product 20?" Zola asked. "Perhaps in 1967?"

Mrs. Buyak laughed at that. "Well, Zola, I don't recall ever hearing of Product 20, but that's a very good question to ask."

"Speaking of Boo Berry, that would explain why Griffin's tongue is always blue when he comes to school every morning," Ethan shouted, causing an eruption of laughter.

Griffin immediately covered up. "Nah, my tongue is blue from sucking on grape blow-pops every morning on the bus ride."

"Wouldn't that make it purple?" Melody asked.

"Okay, boys and girls, there's way too much chit chat going on this morning," Mrs. Bowden spoke up. "Let's turn our attention back to Mrs. Sevick, please."

"We're just about out of time for this session, but we are going to take everything out of the

Splat!

time capsule and give at least four items to every single classroom," our principal explained. "Then, I want each class to get into their tribes and research the items you are given and do some sort of oral or written report on it. I think your teachers can discuss it and then perhaps we can have an assembly and have all of the students present their findings on those items when we are finished. It will be a great learning experience for us to see what life was like back in 1966."

Mr. Federici then began clapping as a signal for all of us to give a round of applause. "Thank you, Mrs. Sevick."

Our principal then smiled as the sound of clapping filled the courtyard. "I'm glad all of you enjoyed this, and I'm sure all of the adults did as well."

I then tugged on Mrs. Sevick's arm to get her attention. "What is the big surprise you have planned for the fourth graders?"

Mrs. Sevick made pretend that she had forgotten, then turned up the microphone. "And now, I would like the fourth graders to stay behind while all of the other grades return to the classroom. The fourth graders are going to have a big barbecue right now on the lower field and then we are going to have our own version of field day with all sorts of fun events and prizes to hand out."

"Awesome," I cried out, pumping my right fist in the air two times. As if this day had not already been totally fantastic, it was now going to get ten times better!

HOT DOG HEAVEN

A few minutes later, the entire fourth grade filed onto the field behind Eli Terry School to see what was in store for us. Although we had no idea about our special field day, we knew that it would bring lots of fun. Every June, Mrs. Sevick arranged a special day for each of the grades that involved all sorts of events and prizes, and I guessed that today was the day for the fourth graders to enjoy.

"Joey, if we get to do an egg toss, then I want to pair up with you," Stephon stated as he ran up beside me.

"Cool, that sounds great to me," I remarked.

"I'm hoping to cream everyone in the fifty-yard dash," Noah declared. "I don't think anyone can run faster than I can."

"No way, Noah," London argued. "Your legs might be longer than mine, but I can outrun anyone. My legs kick butt."

Hannah was quick to break up the friendly competition. "Look, you guys, we'll just have to wait and see who wins today, but don't be surprised if a girl can outrun either of you."

"Yeah, that's right," Mandy pointed out. "You boys have nothing on us girls."

Over at the far side of the field, I noticed my teacher setting up a big barbecue grill with the school janitor. "Hey, Mr. Federici, what are you doing over there?"

Andre J. Garant

Our teacher pulled a large white chef's hat on his head before smiling at me. "Well, Joey, someone has to feed all of you hungry fourth graders today. How does a nice hamburger and a hot dog sound to you for lunch a little later on?"

"Dude, that would be awesome," I cried out while rubbing my belly which was now growling like a cement mixer on high speed.

"Well, then let me fire this thing up and we'll get your growing body fed in a little while. I think Mrs. Buyak is going to make you guys run a bit first."

As if on cue, Mrs. Buyak blew a whistle on the far side of the field and turned on her megaphone. "Okay, I need all fourth graders over here, please." At once, all sixty-five of us ran over to see what she had planned. "As you may have guessed, boys and girls, today is going to be Eli Terry's fourth grade field day and we're also going to have a few other fun events for you to enjoy."

"Like what?" Sierra cried out.

"Be quiet and she'll tell us," Matt barked.

"Can we do an egg toss today?" Jacob S. asked with a smile. "I just love egg tosses, and especially when your challenger gets egg yolk all over his face."

Christopher laughed out loud. "Yeah, nice, slimy and yellow egg yolk running down your face and into your mouth. Yummy, yum, yum."

"You're crazy, Christopher," Brianna D. stated with a frown. "Who would want to taste egg yolk?"

Before anyone could answer, Mrs. Buyak spoke into the megaphone. "Well, it just so happens that we are planning an egg toss among a few other

Splat!

activities. I'll bet you guys would also like to have a hot dog eating contest."

"Oh, boy," Alexander cried out. "I would love that. I'll bet I can eat more hot dogs than anyone in the entire fourth grade."

"No way, dude," Donny argued. "I can beat anyone at Eli Terry fair and square. I might not be that big, but my stomach can hold a ton of food without throwing up."

Mrs. Bowden was quick to explain the rules to us. "Boys and girls, you will be limited to three hot dogs each but the first prize goes out to who can get them down the fastest."

"With or without throwing them up?" Jacob L. asked.

Mrs. Buyak laughed out loud. "Well, we didn't exactly think about that, but perhaps we should make it *without* throwing up. I don't think any of us want to see you getting sick."

Jared wagged a finger at our reading instructor. "Mrs. Buyak, you should know that throwing up is a very important part of an eating contest."

Meg disagreed at once. "Since when, Jared? Maybe for the boys it is, but us girls can eat three hot dogs without throwing up, without burping, and without making a big scene."

Sean G. chuckled. "Yeah, and then you wipe your little mouths with your nice little napkins, too."

"The heck with that," Stefan shouted out. "I'll just wipe my mouth on my arm like I always do."

Grace sneered. "That's gross, Stefan! Didn't your mother ever teach you any manners?"

CJ nodded his head. "Yup, my parents taught

Andre J. Garant

me manners, like not to burp or pass gas at the dinner table, but do you think I pay attention to manners when I'm in school?"

Garrett laughed. "Yeah, tell me about it, guys. The only time I use manners at the dinner table is when we go to my grandmother's house for Thanksgiving dinner."

Mrs. Bowden merely shook her head. "Why am I not surprised, boys? I mean, I have two boys at home and they're no different."

London merely grinned from ear to ear. "Well, Mrs. Bowden, boys will be boys."

"Don't remind us," Camille said, although grinning as she did. "Us girls see it every single day of our lives."

Mr. Federici then walked up to us with a big smile on his face. "Okay, who wants to eat some hot dogs?"

At once, a giant rumble of kids began jumping up in the air and raising their hands, wanting to take part in the hot dog contest.

Being that I was slightly taller than the rest of my classmates, I jumped as high as I could so as to be seen. "Me, me, please pick me."

Mr. Federici began picking students by pointing at them. "How about if we take groups of five, and we'll do the girls first."

"Yes, that's because we're awesome," Ashley cried out.

"Fine, that way us boys can learn from their mistakes," Aaron declared.

The five girls to take part in the hot dog eating contest were Camryn, Dakota, Jenny, Madison, and Sydney.

Splat!

"I'm placing my bet on Madison," Zach declared. "I'll bet she can eat the most hot dogs."

"No way, Zach," Jonathan argued. "I'm going with Sydney."

The girls lined up near the table that our janitor had set up and took their places as each one received a plate with three hot dogs on it.

"Okay, you can put any type of condiments you want on your hot dogs, but keep in mind that might just slow you down a bit when you eat them. It's also more food in your stomach," Mr. Federici explained.

"That's exactly why I don't want anything on my dogs," Dakota explained.

Mr. Federici waited patiently while Camryn and Jenny put some condiments on their hot dogs. At the same time, all of the remaining fourth graders crowded around as close as possible so as to get an up-close view of the activities. It was all very exciting!

"Okay, everyone, on the count of three, you can start eating your hot dogs. You must swallow the entire contents down. There is no leaving anything in your mouth," Mr. Federici called out. "On your mark; one, two, THREE."

At once, the girls started chowing down on their hot dogs as the rest of us began cheering and screaming for them. Each of us picked our victors, but it was a very close contest right up to the end.

"Go, Camryn, go," Jacob W. shouted in his loudest voice. "You only have one measly hot dog left."

"You can do it, Dakota," Maria screamed. "I'm counting on you."

Andre J. Garant

"I want Jenny to win," John hollered, pumping his fists in the air for emphasis.

It was a dead-even contest as all five girls struggled to finish their third hot dog, but Dakota appeared to be winning by a small margin as she quickly chewed her final hot dog and prepared to swallow it down the hatch.

"Come on, Dakota, you're almost there," Brianna H. screamed at the top of her lungs. "I know you can do it."

In the nick of time with only a second to spare, Dakota slammed her hand down on the table and opened her mouth to show that she had swallowed the last hot dog. She was the winner!

"Congratulations, Dakota," Mrs. Buyak called out in her megaphone. "Boys and girls, we have a winner."

"Ugh, I think I'm going to be sick," Jenny cried out as she spat the rest of her hot dog onto the grass. "I just cannot eat any more of this stuff."

Dakota merely smiled and began hugging some of her friends while a few of the boys gave her high fives. "Wow, I can't believe I just did that. I've never eaten three hot dogs in my entire life all at once like that."

"Are you going to yack your brains out now?" Jason asked with a huge smile on his face, sounding as if he wanted to see it happen.

"Yeah, let's see you puke up those hot dogs," Brandon cried out before busting out in a fit of laughter.

"Stop it! You guys are not being nice to her," Erin shouted while pushing the boys away from Dakota. "Don't listen to them. They're just being silly fourth graders."

Splat!

"How else would you expect us to act?" Jonathan asked while throwing his hands up in the air for emphasis.

"Okay, do we have five boys who would like to take part in the contest?" Mr. Federici called out, knowing all too well that it was indeed a very silly question. At once, it was like a stampede as every single one of the fourth grade boys ran up to the table and started pushing and shoving at one another. "Easy does it, guys. Let's calm down."

"I want to be in the contest," Connor cried out.

"Yeah, me too," Maxim hollered.

I jumped up and down so as to get my teacher's attention, but it was too late as he had already picked out the five contestants, who were Adrian, Billy, Connor, Maxim, and Sean D.

"Dudes, I'm voting for Billy all the way," Sean H. called out.

"Not me, I'm putting my bet on Connor," Ethan yelled.

"You guys obviously have never seen me eat hot dogs before," Billy shouted. "I can eat about ten of them in a row without puking."

"I'd like to see that," Alexandra pointed out. "But maybe we should wait for a time when I have my camera so we can make it official."

"Speaking of cameras, I'm taking pictures of this great event for all of us to enjoy later on," Mrs. Bowden stated. "We can put them up in our wall of fame for next year's students to see."

Cassidy cleared her throat. "Um, don't you mean our wall of *shame*, Mrs. Bowden?"

Griffin cracked up laughing. "Yeah, like we

really want this year's third graders to see us puking up hot dogs."

"So far nobody has gotten sick," Mrs. Buyak stated. "I have to say I'm impressed."

"Can we eat more than three hot dogs?" Maxim asked while rubbing his stomach. "I'm kind of hungry right now. Besides, I can easily eat three just for a midnight snack."

Mr. Federici chuckled. "Let's just stick to three dogs, buddy. You can have more for dinner when you get home tonight."

At once, the five boys stood up near the table and took their places, now anxious to show off their hot dog eating abilities to the rest of their classmates. I was a bit bummed out that I wasn't one of them since I knew I could polish off three hot dogs in a flash.

"Hold up, I'm not ready yet," Adrian called out as he was busy smearing oodles of ketchup on his hot dogs.

"Yeah, me neither," Sean D. insisted while he doused his dogs with gobs of green relish and yellow mustard.

Mr. Federici waited for each of the boys to finish up their final preparations as he glanced at his watch. "Okay, boys, on your mark, get set, GO!" At once, all five boys began inhaling their hot dogs like a pack of hungry wolves as the rest of us cheered and hollered for them. Maxim got behind for a few seconds as he dropped his second hot dog on the ground, leaving a trail of sticky ketchup down the front of his tee shirt, but quickly caught up as he literally stuffed the grass-coated hot dog into his mouth and swallowed it whole.

"Go, Billy, go," Sean H. hollered as he watched

Splat!

his friend stuff his second hot dog into his mouth, smearing gobs of ketchup and mustard all over his lips.

"Come on, Connor, you can do it," Ethan screamed while jumping up and down with an endless supply of energy. Although Connor was lagging a bit behind, he quickly caught up as he nearly gagged on the chewed up mass of meat and bread he stuffed down his throat with his fingers.

As it came close to the end, Adrian appeared to take the lead as he started forcing his third hot dog into his mouth with incredible speed. He wasn't even chewing anything at all, but merely shoving it down his throat.

"I think Adrian's going to win it," Jack shouted in his loudest voice as he slammed his hand on the table.

"And we have a winner," Mrs. Buyak shouted into the megaphone as Adrian clearly came back from behind and was the proclaimed winner as he opened up his mouth and showed us that he had miraculously swallowed his last hot dog in one quick gulp.

"That was awesome, Adrian," Jimmy cried out before slapping his pal on the back.

Adrian merely smiled and lifted his arms high over his heads. "Dudes, I'm in hot dog heaven right now."

Mr. Federici was clearly impressed. "Wow, Adrian, I'm amazed you did that. You were behind for a while and it even looked like you were in last place for a few seconds, but you clearly came through and took the lead. How did you do that?"

Andre J. Garant

Adrian just smiled and shook his head. "I don't know, I just forced everything down my throat."

"Do you feel like puking right now?" Eric asked.

"Not one bit," Adrian answered as he received pats on the back from all of his classmates.

"All of you did a spectacular job with the hot dogs," Mrs. Buyak called out. "Let's give everyone a big round of applause." With that said, the entire field behind Eli Terry School erupted in shouts of happiness and cheering as we all clapped our hands. It really was a fun event to watch.

"Can we do some more?" Justin asked, eager to try his luck at eating three hot dogs.

"Sorry, buddy, but we only prepared thirty hot dogs for the contest, so they're all gone now. The rest are for our lunchtime barbecue," Mr. Federici answered.

"Aw, man, I wanted to see someone puke up," Ryan remarked.

"What is it with boys and their fascination with puking?" Melody asked in a disgusted tone.

"You find the answer to that and please let me know," Mrs. Bowden declared with a smile. "I've been teaching kids for years and still don't know the answer to that question."

All of us just started laughing as we enjoyed the finish of our first event, but knowing the fun was only beginning on our special day at Eli Terry School.

JAKE TAKES THE CAKE

We were all very excited to find out what our next event of the day was, and according to Mrs. Sevick, it was a new event that we had never done before.

"Mrs. Sevick, please tell us what we are doing next," Mandy insisted.

Our principal simply smiled as we walked behind her over to the far edge of the athletic field where two large tables were set up. We immediately noticed that there was a large box placed on top of the table which we recognized right away as something from a bakery.

"Hey, that looks like a cake to me of some sort," Geena proclaimed.

"Are we going to have cake now?" Ethan asked as his eyes bugged out in his head. "Oh boy, lots of yummy cake for my tummy."

Mrs. Sevick began laughing at Ethan's antics as she patted him on top of his head. "Dear Ethan, you are such a handful, but a very cute one at that."

"He certainly is a handful," Mrs. Bowden remarked while rolling her eyes. "Try teaching him for six hours straight and then see just how cute he is."

Ethan appeared to be somewhat insulted. "Sticks and stones may break my bones, but words will never hurt me."

"Oh, sweetie, you know by now I'm only kidding

Andre J. Garant

you, right?" Mrs. Bowden remarked as she gave her student a warm hug. "I'm going to miss you so much when the summer comes."

"Miss him?" London chirped before sneering. "The only thing I'll miss about Eli Terry is recess every day."

"Boys and girls, let's have a little appreciation for our school and our wonderful teachers," Mrs. Sevick called out. "I know it's the end of the year and you are all excited to get out for the summer, but before you know it, fifth grade will be knocking on your door with lots more homework."

"Please don't use that awful word," Summer cried out.

"What word, homework?" Hannah asked.

Jason sighed deeply and answered for everyone. "Yes, homework. It's a very nasty eight-letter word that makes me cringe every time I hear it."

Mrs. Buyak chuckled. "You kids are on a roll today. I think you all have a bad case of spring fever."

"Bring it on," Sean G. shouted. "Spring fever all the way, dudes."

Mrs. Bowden cleared her throat to get everyone's attention. "Okay, boys and girls, let's listen to what Mrs. Sevick has to say now, please."

Our principal then began explaining the very new event at Eli Terry School, which was that of decorating a giant cake that we would eventually eat after lunch. "What you are going to do is take turns decorating the cake with icing and decorations, and then after we are done, we will eat it for dessert."

CJ's face twisted into a frown. "Can we write anything we want on it?"

Splat!

Mrs. Sevick held up a finger. "Ah, good question, honey. The answer is 'no'. You must write things on the cake that you remember from the time capsule this morning."

"Say what?" Jonathan blurted out, causing everyone to giggle.

"What she means is that we need to think of stuff that we saw in the time capsule and write it on the cake so that we'll remember it," Meg stated to the entire class.

Mrs. Buyak nodded her head. "Well done, sweetie. Yes, that is exactly what we need to do today, kids. I want this to be a learning experience for all of you. The time capsule we opened up this morning has lots of important history in it that you will need to think about for your oral or written report you are going to prepare before school lets out."

"I kind of liked that Tang stuff," Anthony remarked. "I'd like to drink some of it and see if it makes my tongue all orangey."

"Yeah, and I'd like to try brushing my teeth with that toothpaste we found in there," Andy declared. "Maybe it will make my teeth nice and white."

"Your teeth already are nice and white," Madison remarked, paying her classmate a rare compliment.

"This is all good stuff to think about, everyone," Mrs. Sevick announced. "Keep doing that and I want you to take turns writing on the cake and let's come up with as many themes and topics that relate to 1966. Who can give us a few more?"

Stefan raised his hand. "Um, how about the

Andre J. Garant

Ford Mustang? It was a very popular car back in that year."

Mrs. Buyak nodded her head. "Excellent, Stefan. Let's have a few more."

"How about the Product 19 cereal that Ainsley picked out of the time capsule?" Griffin questioned. "It looked pretty gross to me, but I guess someone ate it back in 1966."

"Well, they certainly didn't have Apple Jacks and Cocoa Puffs back then," Camille declared. "We are so lucky to be growing up in 2011 and not 1966 when kids our age had to eat that yucky Product 19."

"But at least they had Tang to drink," Donny stated. "That stuff sounds pretty good to me. I wonder if it can still be bought in stores."

"I don't think so, Donny," Mr. Federici answered. "But you guys have all sorts of other nice drinks today that were not around forty-five years ago."

"How about remembering some of the prices of things back in 1966," Mrs. Sevick called out, wanting us to jog our memories. "Joey, do you remember any prices of things back then?"

I nodded my head. "Yup, I remember that movie tickets only cost around one dollar and they cost around eight dollars today."

"And what do we call that, kids, when the prices of things go up over time?" Mrs. Bowden asked the entire class.

Jared was quick to show off his broad knowledge. "It's called inflation."

"Okay, you guys get the picture," Mrs. Sevick stated. "I want you to keep thinking of things and take turns going up to the cake in groups of four

Splat!

to decorate. Do your best job so that we can make this a learning experience."

Brianna D. raised her hand. "Mrs. Sevick, aren't we supposed to not eat cake here at Eli Terry School?"

Our principal nodded her head with a smile. "Great question, honey, and the answer is not very often. But today is a special day for us and we can all enjoy a nice piece of cake to celebrate our fourth graders. If anyone cannot eat cake, then we have healthy snacks for you to enjoy."

"Oh, I can eat cake, all right, in fact several pieces at a time," Jacob L. announced to everyone as he pushed out his stomach so that it protruded against his tee shirt.

Mrs. Sevick couldn't help but chuckle. "Oh, you guys are just making me laugh today. This is a reminder of why I love fourth graders so much."

"It's because we're the cutest, brightest, and funnest students of all," Noah declared.

"You mean the most fun," Mrs. Bowden stated as she ruffled Noah's mop of brown hair. "And if you behave, then I'll agree that you're cute as well."

"Mrs. Bowden, there has to be a reason why you love to teach fourth graders so much," Sierra pointed out. "I think it's because we're just the best kids of all, end of story."

Our teacher was quick to agree. "Well, I think you are right, Sierra. The first graders just weren't cutting the mustard for me."

Zach scratched his chin. "Hmm, cutting the mustard, that's a weird saying. Do you really need to cut mustard? Anytime I have seen it, it comes out of the container as a liquid."

Andre J. Garant

"It's kind of like cutting the cheese," John hollered, causing everyone to screech with laughter. "I never need to cut mine with a knife, it just comes out all by itself."

"Oh, my, we've created a bunch of monsters here at Eli Terry," Mrs. Buyak exclaimed before everyone started laughing even harder.

After the giddiness and excitement of the cake wore off a bit and we had all taken turns writing our decorations on the chocolate frosting, the end result was pretty neat. Mr. Federici took several digital pictures of us posing near the cake to show off our decorations. Grace was a talented artist and had managed to draw a picture of a Ford Mustang with the icing while Maxim attempted to draw a picture of Elvis Presley in a white suit, even if the head got all botched up at the end. All in all, our 1966 cake was now complete and we had all learned a bit of history at the same time.

In order to get a really nice picture of the cake with everyone around it, our school janitor offered to climb up on a ladder and take a picture from above so that the entire cake was visible with all the students around each side. It seemed like a great idea for the yearbook, but it took oodles of time for the teachers to get everyone in order without pushing and shoving and all that nonsense that fourth graders like to do. I could swear on my life that Zola kept trying to tickle me as we stood next to each other, but I refused to laugh for fear that she might think I was ticklish and do it even more. Boy oh boy!

"Okay, boys and girls, let's get nice and quiet now and continue to smile for the picture," Mrs. Sevick announced. "I don't want any more

Splat!

horseplay until the pictures are done. After this, we are going to have our field day competition and get you all tired out for lunch."

"Yeah, I can't wait to run the fifty-yard dash," London cried out.

"And I want to do the long jump," Christopher hollered.

"Boys, that's enough," Mrs. Bowden stated in a firm tone, causing more muffled giggles from the rest of the boys.

I was standing in the very front of the table, almost right in front of the cake. To my left was Zola and on my right was Jake who was holding a few items from the time machine to give the picture a real feel from 1966.

"Okay, everyone, here we go," our janitor declared as he began taking pictures about eight feet up in the air. He was standing on a rickety old ladder that began creaking and moaning as the janitor shifted his weight to take the pictures.

"Dudes, I think that ladder is going to give out," Jake whispered to nobody in particular, and before I could say anything, the ladder suddenly collapsed and the janitor came tumbling down right for Jake.

"Jake, get out of the way," Ashley screamed, but it was of no use. The poor boy tried to turn away from the janitor, but the man came hurling down and struck Jake right on his back, sending the boy sprawling face first into the massive chocolate cake! It all happened so fast that nobody said a word for about ten seconds before Mr. Federici rushed over to pull the janitor off of Jake. By the time we got our classmate out from under all the muck, it was clear to see that he was perfectly

Andre J. Garant

fine, even if his face and shirt were smothered with chocolate frosting.

"Hey, guys, the cake is pretty good," Jake merely spoke as he started to lick his lips to get all the frosting off.

"Let me taste some," Jason shouted as he ran up to his brother and began scooping gobs of the frosting off Jake's shirt and licking it from his fingers.

Not to be left out of the action, Jimmy then ran up and began tasting some of the gobs of cake that stuck to Jake's shirt. "Mmm, this cake is yummy stuff."

Mrs. Sevick started laughing when she saw the three triplets feasting on Jake's shirt. "Now, that's a picture, everyone." The rest of us joined in the laughter, even the three twins as we all watched them tasting the cake and making a meal from Jake's shirt and his hair which was still all coated over with chocolate frosting.

Jake then slung his arms around his two brothers and pulled them in tight. "We're the three musketeers, everyone."

"You guys probably taste like a three musketeers bar right now, too," Alexander squealed as he watched Jake wipe thick gobs of chocolate frosting all over Jason and Jimmy's face, causing us to laugh even harder. It was one of those moments that just made everything seem right with the world, you know the ones where a kid feels all warm and fuzzy inside? I wanted fourth grade to last forever at Eli Terry School! With all of my friends and wonderful teachers around me, it was easily the best year of my life so far!

Mr. Garant's books = ???
Postage Stamps = 5 cents each
Average Income = $6,900 per year
Harvard University = $1,760 per year
Apartment Rent = $120 per month
Ground Hamburger = 45 cents per pound

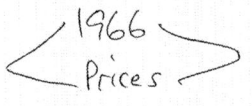

1966 Prices

New House = $14,175
New Car = $2,653
Movie Ticket = $1.25
Gasoline = 32 cents per gallon
Vitamin D Milk = $1.11 per gallon
Ground Coffee = 90 cents per pound
Eggs = 36 cents per dozen
Fresh Bread = 22 cents per loaf

1966 Foods

Product 19 cereal — Boring cereal for a 4th grader! No Boo Berry or Count Chocula!

TANG — what astronauts drank. Good stuff (turns the tongue orange)

SEGO Liquid Diet Food ← sucky!

Sunbeam White Bread — makes great French Toast

Swanson TV Dinner
- yummy crispy fries
- Blueberry muffin
- Peas in butter sauce
- Meatloaf (yum)
- Gravy

Floss your teeth!   Rinse your mouth!   Brush After Meals!

1966 Toothpaste!

[Super] Stripe ANTI-CAVITY
FLUORIDE TOOTHPASTE

- Reduces Cavities
- Prevents Tooth Decay
- Makes your Dentist happy

Don't eat too many snacks!

Fahrenheit 451   Lyndon B. Johnson

Montreal Canadiens   Katherine Anne Porter   Billy Casper

Sinead O'Connor   Product 19

Tang   The Wonder of

Michigan State   GE   1966   Super Stripe

Batman   Deborah Bryant   Notre Dame

Jackie Gleason TV Show   Pet Milk

The Beach Boys   Gomer Pyle   Mike Tyson

Green Acres   Amana   The Lovin' Spoonful

Steve Spurrier

Hubert Humphrey   Palmolive Gold   Frigidaire

Royal Typewriters   Ford

WE'RE ALL WINNERS!

After our little cake episode with Jake, James, and Jason had finally worn off, we were all excited to find out what our next event was going to be. Not even five seconds had passed before Mr. Federici turned on his megaphone.

"Okay, boys and girls, we now have some good old-fashioned field day events for you to enjoy, and we've already put your names in a hat and pulled them out to learn who will be doing what."

"Oh, boy, I hope I'm going to do the long jump this year," Jared announced.

"And I really want to do the tug of war," Eric remarked.

Mr. Federici waited for all of us to calm down, which was quite an amazing event considering school was almost over for the year and we were all majorly excited about moving up to fifth grade in just a few months. "The first event will be the fifty-yard dash and we are going to have Sean D., Aaron, Joey, Brianna H., Garrett, Dakota, Jacob S., Melody, Sydney, and Jenny."

"Aw, man, but I wanted to do that this year," Jonathan cried out.

I slapped my friend on the back. "You can just root for me this time since I'm going to win this event."

"I wouldn't count on it, Joey," Melody warned me as she wagged a finger in my direction.

Andre J. Garant

"I'm betting on Jacob," Noah declared. "After all, he has the fastest legs in the fourth grade."

"Maybe so, but I can probably still beat him," Dakota stated with authority.

"Okay, those of you are who are in the fifty-yard dash, let's get lined up over at the starting line," Mrs. Bowden called out. "We have to keep things moving this morning."

I ran over with the rest of the kids and took my place in between Sean and Garrett. "Dudes, it's time for me to kick some butt here at Eli Terry."

Garrett merely shook his head and laughed at me. "Dream on, Hence. This race is mine."

Mr. Federici held the megaphone to his mouth. "On your mark, get set, GO!" In less time than you could spit (which is not much time!), we were off like a shot, running down the field. Mrs. Buyak was waiting down at the far end to see who crossed the finish line first. Being that I had some pretty long legs, I sprinted with all my might and took the lead for a short time, then Jenny came charging ahead. Then it was Brianna's turn to show her stuff, and by the time we all came closer to the finish line, it seemed as if everyone was going to arrive at the same time.

"Come on, everyone, you can do it," Mrs. Bowden called out as she cheered us on.

I pushed with all my might, feeling my legs burn a bit as I gave the race everything I had. At the last nano-second, Jacob sprinted forward and crossed the line first as the long ribbon broke across his chest.

"You did it, Jacob, you won the race," Anthony shouted as he pumped his fists in the air. "You rock, dude."

Splat!

"Thanks, buddy," Jacob panted as he slapped his friend a couple of high fives. "It was real easy."

"How did you do that, Jacob?" Sydney asked her classmate as he merely shrugged off all the attention everyone gave him.

"Piece of cake, Sydney. I just saved up my energy for the last second, then pushed as hard as I could. That's the secret to winning any race."

"I think he's right," Mr. Federici agreed. "A good contestant always lets his opponents use up their energy first while he saves his up for the very last minute."

"But you're all winners to us today, so each one of you gets a blue ribbon," Mrs. Sevick stated as she started passing out blue ribbons to each of us who had taken part in the fifty-yard dash.

"Do I get a gold star on my ribbon since I came in first place?" Jacob asked, giving our principal his best puppy eyes to win her affection.

"Oh, Jacob, I couldn't possibly give you enough gold stars for all the great work you did this year here at Eli Terry," Mrs. Sevick stated as she ruffled the boy's mop of brown hair.

"Great job, pal," Mr. Federici stated as he patted Jacob's back. "But, like Mrs. Sevick just said, each one of you is a winner to us, not just Jacob."

"Speaking of winners, I once heard a great saying," Camille pointed out. "A winner never quits, and a quitter never wins."

"Oh, Camille, that was wonderful," Mrs. Buyak remarked. "That is so true when you stop to think about it."

"My mother always tells me that I'm a winner

Andre J. Garant

as long as I try my best at everything I do," Ashley said. "I think it really works."

"Excellent point, sweetie," Mrs. Bowden insisted. "I want all of you to remember that."

"Okay, what's our next event?" Ethan asked, wanting to keep the events moving along.

Mr. Federici glanced down at his clipboard. "Up next we have the long jump, and this year we have Matt, Sean H., Billy, Jacob W., Adrian, Zola, Maria, Erin, Camryn, and Alexandra."

"Whoo-hoo, I love the long jump," Maria cried out. "I hope I win this year."

Mrs. Bowden waved us over. "Come on, fourth graders. The sand pit awaits your arrival for the long jump."

I ran over with the rest of the boys and got a perfect spot to watch the jumpers. I secretly hoped that Billy would win since I knew he was a really good jumper. He may have been one of the shorter kids in our class, but he could really jump! Then again, Zola would definitely give him a run for his money.

"Okay, let's have our contestants line up," Mrs. Buyak instructed. "I think we should alternate boy girl, boy girl."

"Then I'll go first," Sean H. stated as he wedged his way to the front. "The best contestant always goes first."

"Not true," Zola admitted as she took her place at the end of the line. "Haven't you heard the saying that the best is always saved for last?"

"Whatever," Sean mumbled as he prepared to jump. Mr. Federici waited patiently with the tape measure. "Geronimo."

"Three feet and ten inches, Sean," Mr. Federici

Splat!

called out as Mrs. Bowden wrote down the measurements on her pad.

"Dude, that so rocked," Sean cried out as he pumped his fist in the air.

Up next was Maria who landed a good two inches ahead of Sean. "Whoo-hoo, Sean, you already got beat by a girl."

"Ha ha," Brandon shouted.

Billy was up next and didn't fare as well as I had hoped. "Three feet and nine inches, Billy," Mr. Federici announced.

"Aw, man, that stunk," Billy said while slumping his shoulders with a look of defeat.

"Remember, Billy, that you are all winners to me," Mrs. Sevick reminded her fourth grade student, which immediately cheered him up.

Alexandra was up next and surprised all of us by jumping four feet, one inch. "Yeah, who says that girls can't jump?"

"If I ever said that, I take it back," Jake said with a smile, a few leftover gobs of frosting still stuck in his blond hair.

Adrian was up next and came in a disappointing last place so far with three feet, eight inches. "Aw, dudes, I want a repeat on that one."

Camryn then dazzled all of us with the best jump yet at four feet, four inches. "Wow, I have no idea how I jumped that far. Did I cheat?"

Everyone busted out laughing. "I don't think so, Camryn," Mrs. Buyak answered. "That looked like a clean jump to me."

"It's because you're small like I am," London pointed out. "We don't weigh all that much, so it's easier to jump farther."

Up next was Matt who was easily one of the

Andre J. Garant

taller kids in our grade, so he had a definite advantage and was able to beat everyone as he jumped four feet, six inches. "All right, dudes, I take the cake on the long jump."

Zola cleared her throat. "Um, it's not over yet, Matt."

"My turn to go," Erin remarked as she took her place and prepared to jump.

"Three feet and ten inches," Mr. Federici called out after measuring where her feet landed.

"I'm the last boy to go," Jacob W. declared. "It's now or never for the boys."

"We're counting on you, Jacob," Sean G. called out. "Kick some butt and take down some names while you're at it."

Jacob had a pretty impressive jump and had come in second place so far. "Not bad, pal," Mr. Federici announced. "That was four feet, five inches."

Jacob raised his arms in victory. "Dudes, that's how tall I was in third grade."

Zola then smiled as she took her place. "Okay, and now the best will do her jump."

"Go, Zola, go," Camille shouted, doing her best job at cheering for her classmate.

We were all amazed when Zola was able to jump a full four feet, eight inches. "Zola wins the long jump, everyone. She jumped four feet, eight inches," Mr. Federici announced with a smile.

At once, Zola was surrounded by all of the girls in the class as they gave her hugs of congratulations. "I have no idea how I did that. I was only kidding when I said I could jump the farthest."

Splat!

"Aw, man, I almost had her beat," Matt mumbled to himself. "I can't believe that."

"Well, believe it because girls are awesome," Sydney stated in a confident tone.

"Girls, girls, girls, they always get all the attention," Christopher admitted.

"I don't know about that, sweetie," Mrs. Sevick declared. "I just gave Jacob S. quite a show of attention when he won the fifty-yard dash. Plus, I think you get an award for being a model fourth grader this year."

"Me?" Christopher asked, looking up at our principal with his big blue eyes.

Mrs. Sevick nodded her head. "Sure thing, kiddo. I've been keeping my eye on you around Eli Terry this year and I must say I've been very impressed by your maturity and willingness to help your teachers and classmates."

Christopher beamed from ear to ear. "It's like you said, Mrs. Sevick, we're all winners to you."

"Like I said earlier, I am going to miss you guys really badly when this year ends," Mrs. Bowden stated.

"You know we're going to miss you, too," Maxim remarked with a smile.

"Okay, guys, let's prepare for the sack race," Mr. Federici announced. "Today's contestants include Madison, Stefan, Zach, Meg, Ryan, John, Donny, Mandy, Sierra, and last but certainly not least, Summer."

"How come it's always five boys and five girls and I never get picked?" Ethan whined while tugging on Mr. Federici's arm.

"Don't worry, pal, your turn will come sooner or later. If not in one of the races, we'll be sure to

Andre J. Garant

get you in on the action today at some point," Mr. Federici answered.

"Let's get you guys in your gunny sacks," Mrs. Bowden called out as the ten contestants ran over to her. "Make sure you try to tie them around your waist so they don't fall down. No cheating today."

Once all ten of the contestants were suited up in their gunny sacks, Mrs. Buyak blew a whistle, sending everyone into action. Poor Donny didn't get more than two feet before he tripped over himself and fell down, which then caused Meg to fall down on top of him.

"Come on, Donny, get up," I shouted. "You're losing."

Zach was in the lead for a short while before he also tripped over his sack and fell sideways, causing Sierra to fall down as well. It was like watching dominos as everyone kept falling into each other and tripping over their feet.

"You can do it, John, keep it up," Jack hollered as he rooted for his friend. It did look like John was going to win the race as he found his rhythm while hopping like a rabbit on both of his feet. "Come on, John."

Madison suddenly came up behind John and bumped into him, causing him to lose balance and fall to the ground. Then Summer bumped into Stefan, causing a four-person pile up on the ground. Donny and Zach were now neck and neck as they hopped towards the finish line with Meg and Sierra close behind.

"Zach, you got it, buddy," Eric hollered, rooting for his close friend. It was a real close call, but Zach finally won the race as he was the first to

Splat!

clear the finish line, followed closely by Donny, Meg, and Sierra. The other four soon lumbered behind, but John took one last spill right before the finish line and simply lay on the ground with his arms outstretched.

"I lose the race," John yelled, trying his best to imitate a wounded soldier. "I should get a prize for coming in last place."

Zach was quickly showered with high fives and pats on the back from all of his buddies as he glowed from ear to ear at being the victor of the sack race. "I can't believe I did that, guys. It felt like I was going to trip every single second."

"You rock, buddy," Eric shouted as he slung his arm around Zach's shoulder and gave his friend a hug.

"Okay, boys and girls, you all get blue ribbons," Mrs. Sevick declared, "and Zachary gets a gold star on his for coming in first place."

"Yahoo," Zach yelled as he pumped his arms in the air and smiled from ear to ear.

"What's next, Mr. Federici?" Jason asked.

"Our last event for this year's fourth grade field day is a giant tug of war and it's going to be boys against girls."

"Awesome," I shouted in my loudest voice.

"That is so cool," CJ hollered. "Now the boys can kick butt and show the girls who's stronger."

Brianna D. hissed at her classmate. "Don't count your chickens before they hatch, CJ. We might just kick *your* butt today."

Andy chuckled. "Ha ha, we'll see about that, Brianna."

"Wait a second," Grace screamed out. "That's

Andre J. Garant

not fair since there are more boys than girls in our class."

Mrs. Buyak raised her hand and smiled. "We already thought of that, kids, and we are going to have all of the teachers join the girls."

"Whoo-hoo, Mrs. Sevick is going to get all muddy today," Jimmy shouted.

"Yeah, hope you plan to get a little wet, Mrs. Buyak," Adrian hollered.

"Be nice, Adrian, or I might have to mark you down on your next reading assignment," Mrs. Buyak shouted back, clearly teasing the boy.

"Okay, everyone, let's take your sides," Mrs. Bowden called out as she got the big rope ready with Mrs. Buyak. At once, all of the boys ran over to my side and the girls got on the other side.

"Now, to make this real interesting today, we're going to spray some water on the dirt to create a little mud pit," Mr. Federici called out as he turned on the hose and sprayed some water on the ground. In between the boys and the girls was a nice dirt pit that soon became rather muddy.

"Awesome," Alexander shouted. "All of the girls are going to go home today with muddy clothes."

"Speak for yourself, Alexander," Cassidy warned.

Griffin then flexed his bicep muscle as he grinned at the girls. "Take a look at this baby, girls! This muscle is going to win us the tug of war today."

"Yeah, my muscles are real strong, too," Jacob L. called out as he did his best to show off for the girls as well.

"What is it with boys always showing off how

Splat!

strong they are?" Ainsley asked with a pouty look on her face.

Mrs. Bowden merely laughed. "I don't know, Ainsley, but maybe you can ask your brother when you get home today. I can honestly tell you that my boys do the same thing."

"Okay, we're ready for the tug of war," Mr. Federici exclaimed as he turned off the hose and admired the nice, muddy puddle he had created. "Boys and girls, take your places in line and get ready for action. On the count of three. One, two, THREE."

I grabbed onto the rope and pulled as hard as I could while gritting my teeth. Aaron was pulling in front of me while Billy was in back. It seemed to be a pretty even match despite Mr. Federici pulling for the girls. Every few seconds the rope would tug forward a few feet, then it would go back a few feet. The hardest part was trying not to fall down on the person in front or in back of you when the rope tugged in any one direction.

"Pull, Jonathan, pull," Justin cried out as he saw the boy getting a little too close to the mud pit.

"I think we've got them," Grace cried out as the rope moved forward a few more inches.

"Come on, guys, I don't want to get my new basketball shirt all muddy today," Garrett muttered through gritted teeth as he struggled to pull us back. We knew it was all over for the boys, however, when Jonathan went sprawling head first into the mud, quickly followed by Sean G., Jared, and London. Stefan and Noah tried to get out of the way, but were shoved forward as Aaron went flying into them, causing all three of them

Andre J. Garant

to fall into the mud puddle. I barely managed to let go of the rope and jump aside, saving Billy and me from falling in along with the rest of the boys behind us.

"We won, we won," Dakota cried out as all of the girls began screaming and cheering. "We told the boys we could beat them."

Jonathan finally crawled out of the mud puddle along with the other boys. "Aww, you only won because you had Mr. Federici pulling in back. If we had him on our side, all of you would have been in that mud."

"Yeah, that tug of war was hardly fair," London complained as he brushed his mud-streaked blond hair out of his face.

"Man, I'm all dirty now," Jared stated with a pained look on his face.

At once, Mrs. Sevick handed a few clean towels to the boys who had managed to fall into the mud puddle. "Sorry, boys, but we thought it would be an even match with the teachers pulling for the girls."

Sean G. threw up his hands as his long brown hair dripped water onto his face. "Ah, what's a little water and mud to a boy? I do this all summer long."

"That's the spirit, Sean," Mrs. Buyak stated as she gave the boy a hug. "You guys did a great job today. Let's get a nice big round of applause for all of our fourth grade winners."

The entire field behind Eli Terry School erupted in cheers and whistles as the boys quickly forgot their loss in the tug of war and realized just how lucky they were to go to such a great school like Eli Terry. After all, our teachers loved us to no end

Splat!

and we all knew it. Like Mrs. Sevick had told us, we were all winners to them, boy or girl, black or white, tall or short, heavy or skinny; they loved each and every one of us!

SPLAT!

After enjoying a great barbecue of hot dogs and hamburgers, all of us thought it was time to return inside for the remainder of the day, but little did we know that we had one last surprise in store for us.

"Okay, guys, I know you're all going to be so bummed out, but Mrs. Sevick and the rest of your fourth grade teachers thought it would be fun to have a first annual egg toss for the fourth graders. What do you guys think?" Mr. Federici asked us.

"Are you kidding me?" Jacob S. shouted out. "Dude, that is so awesome."

"Yeah, and Joey said I could pair up with him, too," Stephon bragged, already making me out to be a winner in egg tossing.

"Wait, is it going to be boys against girls again?" Sydney asked our teacher.

Mrs. Buyak decided to answer. "Nope, kids, you can pair up with whomever you'd like. We thought of doing it quickly, however, and we'd like all of you to go at once and us teachers will be the judges. If the egg breaks in your hands, you are disqualified."

"That's right," Mrs. Bowden chimed in. "We have thirty eggs, so that's enough for each group to go once."

"What does the winner get?" Matt asked while smiling.

Andre J. Garant

"You need to ask?" Mrs. Sevick stated. "Why, a nice blue ribbon with a gold star on it."

Jacob W. chuckled. "Aww, geez, we should have figured that one out since it's all we've been getting all day long."

"Hey, what's wrong with that?" Mrs. Buyak asked, sounding insulted.

Garrett shrugged his shoulders and answered for everyone. "A blue ribbon isn't necessarily bad, but a fourth grader would much rather gobble down a nice hot fudge sundae."

"Yeah, with gobs of caramel sauce and lots of nuts on it, too," Alex remarked.

Mrs. Sevick laughed out loud. "Boy, you guys sure do like your sweets. Perhaps we can have a sundae bar before the end of the school year."

Dakota shook her head. "I don't know, Mrs. Sevick, it's not a healthy snack."

"My dentist will love it," Jake stated. "He always smiles when me and my brothers show up in his office since it means mega moolah for him."

Mrs. Bowden seemed amused. "Why, do you guys have lots of cavities or something?"

Jimmy decided to answer. "Not really, but we sure don't miss out on any snacks."

Mr. Federici brought us back to the egg toss since time was running short. "That's great, guys, we'd love to stay all day and talk about the dentist and ice cream sundaes, but let's get paired up with a partner right now. I'm sure you all know whom you want to do the egg toss with, right?"

"I'm with Joey," Stephon bragged as he slung his arm around my shoulder. "We're gonna kick some heiny today."

Mrs. Bowden merely smiled. "Oh, boy, summer

Splat!

cannot come quick enough. All these big fourth grade words are causing my brain to go into overload."

A few minutes later when everyone had paired up with a partner, Mrs. Sevick began passing out an egg to one of the tossers in each group. "Nobody starts until everyone has an egg and Mr. Federici has explained the rules."

CJ was standing alongside of me as he was paired up with Brandon. "What kind of rules are there in an egg toss, Joey?"

I shrugged my shoulders. "Beats me."

Once every group had an egg, Mr. Federici spoke into his megaphone. "Okay, everyone starts at exactly ten feet apart. With each successful catch, you move back about two feet. Mrs. Sevick, Mrs. Bowden, and Mrs. Buyak will help you to gauge the distance. You keep tossing the egg until it breaks and then you are disqualified. We will keep going until we have the last team."

"That's going to be us, Joey," Stephon spoke from where he stood ten feet across from me.

"I know the perfect technique to catching the egg without making it crack open, but I'm not going to tell you guys," Brandon bragged.

"Maybe I know it, too," I stated before sticking my tongue out at Brandon.

"Okay, is everyone ready?" Mr. Federici asked. Everyone yelled that they were ready. "On your mark, get set, GO."

"Nice and easy, Stephon," I said as I watched my partner gently toss the egg in my direction. I cupped the palms of my hands together and made an easy catch. "Perfect throw, dude. Just keep doing it like that and we'll be winners in no time."

"Not if we can help it," CJ declared as he caught his egg from Brandon with a perfect catch as well.

In less than a minute, the first five teams were eliminated as they had already broken their egg. With each passing minute, another few teams were disqualified and before you knew it, we were down to six groups, three of them girls and three of them boys. Believe it or not, two of the three groups of boys were me and Stephon and CJ and Brandon. The other group was Andy and Billy. For the girls, the three remaining teams were Camryn and Melody, Erin and Brianna H., and Maria and Hannah.

"Throw it easier, Maria," Hannah cried out as she barely caught her egg without it breaking.

"Dude, don't lob the egg so high in the air," Andy shouted to Billy, who was now about twenty-five feet away from him.

"Let's try and make it a little harder, kids," Mrs. Sevick called out. "Why not try throwing the egg a bit higher."

"But it's hard to catch it like that with the sun shining in the sky," Melody called out before successfully making another catch.

"Sounds good to me, Stephon," I shouted. "Let's try a few lobs, shall we?"

"Sure, Joey," Stephon called back to me.

Suddenly, a loud scream caught our attention when Camryn missed the throw from Melody, knocking them out of the tournament. The egg had landed all over her arms, making a yellow, slimy mess of them. The next group to lose was

Splat!

Maria and Hannah when Hannah missed the throw from Maria altogether and the egg cracked open upon hitting the ground.

"Wow, we still have three teams of boys and one team of girls left," Mrs. Bowden cried out. "Great job, everyone."

"It ain't over till it's over," Billy called out just before he made a tremendous catch now standing about thirty feet away from Andy.

"Awesome catch," Andy cried out as he prepared to follow suit.

"Joey, you're throwing them real high, dude," Stephon warned me. "It's almost too high."

"Come on, Joey, you can do it," Sean D. cried out, clearly rooting for our team.

"I want CJ and Brandon to win," Sean H. hollered, and just as he said that, Brandon lost his concentration and the egg split open upon hitting him in the chest.

"Aw, man, that just made me mess up," Brandon yelled out, clearly upset at missing his catch.

"Okay, only two teams of boys and one team of girls remain," Mr. Federici called out. "Who will get the blue ribbon with the gold star?"

Erin suddenly screamed as she slipped in the grass and missed her catch from Brianna H., "Oh, my God, I cannot believe I just slipped like that."

"You guys are out," Connor hollered while pumping his fist in the air. "Only the boys are left in the game."

"Wow, the contest is now literally in the hands of four boys; Andy and Billy or Joey and Stephon," Mrs. Buyak shouted. "Who's going to win it?"

Andre J. Garant

At once, all of our classmates began cheering and yelling for who they wanted to win. It was either one team or the other.

"Andy, Billy," the chants sounded from approximately thirty fourth graders standing at the edge of the field.

"Joey, Stephon," the remainder of our classmates shouted.

"Darn, I can't concentrate with all that yelling," I muttered to myself as I prepared to make another catch from Stephon who was now standing nearly forty feet away from me. With amazing precision, I cradled the egg in my fingertips, trying to absorb as much of the impact as possible. It appeared that Andy was doing the very same thing as he stood about ten feet to my right and continued to make every catch that came his way as well.

"Joey, I'll give you my chocolate chip cookies if you win today," Griffin hollered as he jumped up and down with excitement.

"Andy, I'll give you one of my top baseball cards from my collection," Jack shouted as many of the fourth grade boys offered up their most precious rewards in anticipation of a sweet victory for their preferred winner.

"Dude, that's too high," Andy yelled over to Billy as he practically missed a catch, but pulled it off just the same.

"Well, you said to throw it really high," Billy shouted back from across the field.

"Come on, Joey, I want you and Stephon to win," Cassidy yelled out, offering her own words of encouragement to us.

"Please, Andy and Billy, just win it already,"

Splat!

Madison cried out. "All this egg catching is making me nervous."

At the very same moment, Andy stepped back and must have tripped on something, for he went sprawling down on his back and the egg hit him right in his shorts, causing a mess of slimy, oozy fluid to make a mess of things. "Aw, man, I can't believe that just happened." Andy was steaming mad at his little mishap, and Billy wasn't too pleased either as he came running over to see what happened.

"Holy cow, that's pretty funny, Andy," Billy muttered to his friend once he saw the damage and started laughing along with the rest of the fourth graders nearby.

"Geez, did the egg have to break right there?" Andy asked before he finally laughed at himself. He was doing his best to brush as much of the slimy egg yolk off his shorts as he could. "Hey, don't take my picture like this or my mother will think I still wet myself at ten years old." The damage was already done, however, as Mrs. Buyak snapped several photos of Andy and his egg yolk mess.

"That one is going in the yearbook, pal," Mr. Federici exclaimed as he even got a few laughs in while glancing over at Andy.

"Since we're the winners of the egg toss, should we keep going until we break the egg?" I asked, a little bit annoyed that nobody was even paying attention to Stephon or me any longer.

"Let's take a vote on it," Mr. Federici answered, and in less than a minute, the verdict was decided that every single fourth grader wanted us to continue until the egg broke.

Stephon and I were starting to get a little risky

Andre J. Garant

now as we tossed the egg much higher on each throw, and we knew it was only a matter of a few more throws before one of us missed a catch.

"No, Stephon, that's too high," I shouted as I lost sight of the egg in the sky as the sun was shining down directly into my eyes. At the last second, I saw it coming right for my face and that's when it happened. *Splat!* The egg broke directly on my nose and the cold, runny yolk immediately seeped into my eyes, up my nose, and into my mouth.

"Dudes, check it out," Justin shouted, pointing his finger right at my face as I struggled to get the yolk out of my eyes. Everyone was laughing so hard by now, including the teachers.

At once, I decided to pretend that I was a monster and began rubbing both of my hands over my face in order to get as much slimy egg yolk on my fingers as possible. "I am the monster of Eli Terry School and I have come to slime you over." My first targets were many of the boys who frantically tried to get away from me, but not before I slimed them over pretty good. Jason took a direct shot of yolk right to his cheek as I flung my hand in his direction and Noah didn't fare much better as I snuck up to him and wiped my fingers all through his hair.

"Aww, dude, you die," Noah furiously shouted once he realized what had happened.

Before things got out of hand, Mr. Federici stopped the nonsense, although it was clear to see that he was enjoying the show quite a bit himself. "Okay, Joey, that's enough now. Let's get you cleaned up." Before I knew what was happening, a towel was thrust into my face and began cleaning

Splat!

up all of the sticky egg yolk. In no time at all, I was as clean as a whistle, not to mention any of the other boys who had become my victims in the attack.

"Let's get a nice round of applause for all of our contestants in the egg toss," Mrs. Sevick stated. "All of you did a great job and I think we will definitely have to do this once again next year."

"It was really fun," Jenny declared. "You should definitely do it with every year's fourth grade class."

"Joey and Stephon, please come here," Mrs. Sevick asked, and once she had us at her side, she gave each one of us a big blue ribbon with a giant gold star in the middle of it. "Congratulations to this year's winners of the egg toss." At once, everyone began cheering and clapping for us, and I had never felt so special in all of my time at Eli Terry. Whether my classmates were boys or girls, each one of them was clapping for me with a big smile on their face which made me feel so proud and happy. It really was times like this when I felt so special and knew that I was loved by so many people. It surely was the best feeling in the whole wide world!

ELI TERRY JEOPARDY

With only two classes to go for the day, our fourth grade teachers still had a few activities planned for us, but now we had moved indoors to do some learning.

"Can't we stay outside and do some more field day stuff?" Ryan asked. "I mean, it's so nice out and all."

"Yeah, it's kind of a bummer that we have to come inside now," Zach added.

Mrs. Bowden raised her hand for silence. "Okay, boys and girls, you have had your fun outside, but now it's time to exercise your minds a bit. With that said, we have planned our own version of Eli Terry Jeopardy."

Jonathan's eyes opened wide in amazement. "You mean we get to act like that dude, Alex Quebec?"

"Oh, I just love watching that show," Grace chimed in. "It's my favorite one."

Mr. Federici then explained the rules to us once we had all calmed down a bit. "What we're going to do is have five of you play. We have already picked the names out of a hat, so it's completely random who gets picked. Whoever earns the most points after fifteen minutes will be the big winner."

"Will there be a championship round where we can win a million dollars?" Donny asked.

"Or win a new BMW?" Jacob L. blurted out.

Mrs. Bowden merely chuckled. "Guys, I don't

Andre J. Garant

think Eli Terry could afford to buy you a new BMW, let alone give out a million dollars."

Aaron merely shook his head. "Let me guess, the winner gets a blue ribbon with a big gold star on it, right?" Everyone laughed out loud.

Ashley held up a finger. "Aaron, I think everyone who plays will get a blue ribbon, not just the winner."

"But the winner has to get something better than that," Christopher argued. "A blue ribbon is not enough."

"What do you suggest, pal?" Mr. Federici asked the fourth grader. "You guys need to give us some suggestions."

"How about a gift certificate to take our family to dinner at Burton's Grill?" Geena asked.

"Umm, have you seen how expensive that place is?" Jacob W. countered. "I went there once for my birthday and it was over the top."

"Yeah, I think something a bit more simple would be in order," Mrs. Buyak mentioned. "Anything at Evergreen Walk might be out of the question."

"Not necessarily," Meg pointed out. "The Coldstone Creamery is there and you could get the winner a gift certificate for ten dollars or something simple like that."

"That's a great idea," Sean G. stated. "I love their ice cream."

"Actually, I have to say that is a pretty good idea indeed, Meg," Mr. Federici added. "We'll see what we can do."

"You must have the prize already picked out, right?" Zola asked.

Mrs. Bowden nodded her head. "We sure do,

Splat!

Zola, and so now, let's announce who the five contestants will be." At once, everyone in the room quieted down as we waited for our teacher to tell us who would be playing Eli Terry Jeopardy. "Okay, the contestants in alphabetical order are Ainsley, Camille, John, Maxim, and Sierra." At once, the entire classroom erupted in cheering and applause.

"Awesome, we have some definite girl power in here right now since we have three girls against two boys," Summer announced. "We're definitely going to kick butt today."

"Not so fast," Alexander objected. "Us boys can definitely hold our own, even if we are down by one."

After the five contestants took their places at the five desks that Mrs. Bowden had arranged in the front of the classroom, it was time to begin the competition. Mr. Federici played the part of Alex Trebek and even tried to imitate his voice which made all of us laugh quite a bit. "Okay, everyone, instead of having you choose categories, we are just going to ask you questions and the amount of points awarded to each question is based on the level of difficulty. Therefore, the first question of our Eli Terry Jeopardy which is worth two hundred points is what year did Eli Terry School become the first all-electric school in Connecticut?"

Camille had her hand raised first. "What is 1965."

"Excellent, Camille, you have two hundred points," Mrs. Buyak called out, our official scorekeeper. "Keep in mind, everyone, that the questions we are asking are all things you have

Andre J. Garant

learned in school this year. We tried to keep all of the questions geared toward either Eli Terry School or South Windsor."

Mr. Federici shuffled through his cards. "The next question is worth four hundred points. How many elementary schools are there in South Windsor?"

Maxim raised his hand. "What is four?"

"Sorry, Maxim, that is incorrect," Mr. Federici stated.

Ainsley raised her hand. "What is five."

"Excellent, Ainsley," Mrs. Buyak called out. "And who can tell me what the names of those five schools are?"

Brianna D. was called on to answer. "It's Pleasant Valley School, Wapping School, Orchard Hill School, Smith School, and of course our own school, Eli Terry."

"Excellent job, Brianna," Mrs. Bowden remarked as she started clapping.

"Okay, the next question counts for two hundred points," Mr. Federici explained. "What product was widely grown in South Windsor, and still is, although to a much lesser extent?"

After a few seconds of hesitation from the contestants, John raised his hand. "What is tobacco."

"Excellent job, John," Mrs. Buyak called out. "Tobacco was widely grown in this area due to our proximity to the Connecticut River and its fertile growing soil. Also, here in the Connecticut River Valley, the summers are quite warm and it's the perfect combination for growing tobacco."

"The next question is quite a bit harder and is worth six hundred points, but we discussed it in

Splat!

class about a month ago," Mr. Federici explained to us. "What other commodity was widely grown in South Windsor?"

Maxim raised his hand. "What is corn?"

Mr. Federici made a pained face. "I'm sorry, Maxim, that is somewhat correct, but not the answer we are looking for."

Max pounded his desk. "Aw, man, I almost had six hundred points."

Sierra then proudly raised her hand. "What is rye."

Mrs. Buyak was clearly impressed. "Excellent, Sierra. We discussed this a few times this year and for those of you with a really good memory, we even talked about the street named after Rye here in South Windsor."

"I know where that is," Billy shouted. "There's a big catering place there where we had our soccer banquet last year."

"Not to rub anything in, Ryan, but the girls have twelve hundred points right now while the boys only have two hundred," Summer pointed out.

Ryan merely slid further down in his chair and pouted. "It's not over yet, Summer."

Mr. Federici then asked the next question to keep things rolling. "Okay, contestants, our next question is worth four hundred points. What is the name of the library here in town that serves as our historical museum?"

At once, Maxim's hand shot up like a rocket. "What is Wood Memorial Library."

"Awesome job, Maxim," Mrs. Buyak declared as she started clapping along with all of the boys. "The boys now have six hundred points."

Andre J. Garant

Ryan now sat a little higher in his chair. "Like I said, Summer, it ain't over till it's over." Everyone laughed at that.

"The next question is worth two hundred points and should be real easy to answer," Mr. Federici pointed out. "Who can tell me what county South Windsor is located in?"

John's hand was the first one to fly up in the air. "Um, what is Hartford County."

"Awesome, John," Mrs. Buyak cried out. "Now the boys are only down by four hundred points. Keep it up."

"Whoo-hoo, the boys rock," Matt shouted as he pumped his fists in the air.

Jared continued with the chants. "Yeah, us dudes are gonna show the girls who rules at Eli Terry Jeopardy."

Erin, who was seated next to Jared, merely giggled. "You are so silly, Jared."

"Okay, now for a hard question that is worth a whopping six hundred points," Mr. Federici declared. "Who can tell me what year Eli Terry was born?"

There was a long period of silence before Ainsley raised her hand. "What was 1775?"

Mr. Federici cringed. "Oh, I'm so sorry, Ainsley, you are only off by a few years."

Suddenly, Maxim's hand shot up. "I've got it. What was 1772."

"Wow, Maxim, I am really impressed today with your thinking," Mrs. Bowden exclaimed. "That was really great."

"Right on the money, Maxim," Mrs. Buyak remarked. "And that gives the boys another six

Splat!

hundred points bringing their total to fourteen hundred putting them ahead of the girls."

John immediately reached over and slapped Maxim a burning high five. "Yeah, dude, I knew we could show up the girls."

"Yeah, we rock," Anthony hollered at the top of his lungs.

Just then, Camille planted her hands on her hips and shook her head from side to side. "Like we said earlier, boys, it ain't over till it's over." At once, the crowd of girls in the classroom began cheering and clapping while the boys merely did their best to hush them.

"No way, us boys are going to kick some major butt today, you just wait," Adrian hollered above the crowd of girls.

Mr. Federici raised his hand to signal that silence was requested. "Okay, let's come back down to earth, everyone. I'm glad you're all having a great time today, but let's remember to have respect for each other. The next question is worth two hundred points. Who can tell me the name of the mall that opened here in South Windsor back in 2003?"

Sierra's hand shot up faster than anyone else's. "What is Evergreen Walk."

"Great job, Sierra," Mrs. Buyak commented. "And that gives the girls another two hundred points making the score dead even."

"Yeah, maybe so, but there are three girls up there and only two boys, so that makes us a bit smarter," Garrett pointed out.

Melody objected at once. "No, it doesn't! It's all just in the luck of the draw and how the questions are answered."

Andre J. Garant

"Yeah, Garrett," Sydney stated. "We're all equally smart."

"That's a very good way of looking at it," Mrs. Bowden said. "Let's not think of one gender being smarter than the other."

"Okay, now it's time for another six hundred point question. Who can tell me what year South Windsor was incorporated as a town?" Mr. Federici asked.

All five contestants looked a bit confused as they dug through the recesses of their minds to find the answer. It was something we had all learned back in the fall and when summer is fast approaching, the average fourth grader has one thing on their mind, and it's *not* history.

Ainsley finally raised her hand. "What is 1845?"

"That's exactly right, Ainsley," Mrs. Buyak stated with a big smile on her face. "It sounded like you took a guess, but you were right on the money."

"Now the girls are ahead again," Sean D. exclaimed. "We can't let them beat us today."

"Okay, everyone, the score is now fourteen hundred for the boys and two thousand for the girls," Mrs. Buyak mentioned. "You are all doing a great job answering these questions."

"And now for another four hundred point question, who can tell me which of the five elementary schools we mentioned earlier is located in the extreme southwest corner of South Windsor. It's a tough one," Mr. Federici pointed out.

Camille raised her hand. "What is Wapping School."

Mr. Federici shook his head. "I'm sorry,

Splat!

Camille, that is not correct, but you were on the right track."

At once, John raised his hand. "What is Pleasant Valley School."

Mrs. Buyak began clapping. "Wow, we have a real friendly competition going this morning. Another four hundred points goes to the boys which brings them only two hundred less than the girls."

Mr. Federici smiled at us. "And now, the toughest question of all is worth one thousand points. Who can tell me the name of the minister who settled in South Windsor and eventually had a school named after him? Again, this is worth one thousand points." Everyone looked very confused, to say the least.

Maxim was the first contestant to raise his hand. "Who was Eli Terry?"

Mr. Federici shook his head. "I'm sorry, Maxim, that was a good guess, but it's not correct."

Sierra then raised her hand. "Who was Philip R. Smith?"

Mr. Federici once again shook his head. "I'm sorry, Sierra, but that is not correct."

Camille then smiled as she raised her hand as fast as possible. "Who was Timothy Edwards."

At once, all of the girls began clapping when they saw the smile spread across Mr. Federici's face. It was clear to see that the girls were going to reign supreme in our jeopardy contest.

"Camille, that was excellent," Mrs. Buyak announced. "And now the girls have a whopping three thousand points and the boys have eighteen hundred."

"Aw, dudes, we may as well give up

Andre J. Garant

already," Jacob S. remarked with a look of pure disappointment on his face. "We'll never catch up now."

Mrs. Bowden shook her head in disagreement. "Never say never, Jacob. There is still a bit of time, although we are almost over."

"Two more questions remain, everyone," Mr. Federici said. "The next question is about geography. For two hundred points, who can tell me the name of the town that forms the northern border of South Windsor?"

John raised his hand faster than a speeding bullet. "What is Ellington."

Mr. Federici shook his head. "I'm sorry, John, that is not correct. Ellington would form the eastern border with us."

Ainsley knew the answer right away. "What is East Windsor."

"Great job, Ainsley," Mrs. Buyak declared. "That gives the girls another two hundred points."

"When you stop to think about it, that makes no sense," Mandy explained. "Why would East Windsor be north of South Windsor. Shouldn't the answer be North Windsor?"

Mrs. Bowden nodded her head. "Logic would say yes, Mandy, but there is no such place as North Windsor."

"Okay, everyone, here is your last question, which is worth six hundred points. You should all know the answer to this one fairly easily. What product did Eli Terry invent and manufacture here in Connecticut?"

Nearly all five hands went up at once, so Mr. Federici picked the one he thought was first. "Okay, John, tell us the answer."

Splat!

"What is the clock."

Mrs. Buyak started clapping. "Great job, boys and girls. You all did an amazing job in our game of Eli Terry Jeopardy. The final score is three thousand two hundred for the girls and two thousand four hundred for the boys. Let's give our five contestants a great big round of applause." Everyone started clapping and cheering.

"Let's hear it for the girls," Dakota cried out when Ainsley and Sierra took their seats with the rest of the class again.

"And let's congratulate Camille for answering the thousand point question," Brianna H. pointed out, causing more applause to sound in the classroom.

"We almost had you guys," Connor stated. "It was close, plus you had an advantage with three girls over our two boys."

"It has nothing to do with that, Connor," Camryn argued. "It's whoever answers the question correctly first."

"You all did a great job," Mr. Federici explained. "The winner of our contest with the most points was a tie between Ainsley and Camille with twelve hundred points apiece. Therefore, each of them gets a thirty dollar gift card to Borders at the Buckland Mall so you can buy some new books."

"Oh, that's great," Ainsley remarked, appearing to be genuinely happy with her gift.

"I can't wait to go there and pick out some new books," Camille said. "I hope my mother can take me today."

"And for the rest of you, we have a nice blue ribbon with a gold star on it," Mr. Federici pointed out as he handed one to John, Maxim, and Sierra.

"Gee, what a surprise, Mr. Federici," John remarked, but smiling as he grabbed the blue ribbon from his teacher. "I'm sure my mother and father will be thrilled when they see this."

"Once again, great job, boys and girls," Mrs. Buyak called out. "I know that I am very excited to see how much you have learned this year, and I'm sure your teachers are as well. Keep up the great work and remember to read as much as possible over the summer."

And so our game of Eli Terry Jeopardy came to a close, just like our fourth grade year at Eli Terry. All in all, I couldn't imagine going to a better school and having such great teachers and awesome classmates!

THE OLDEN DAYS

Mrs. Buyak called us to order. "Okay, everyone, it's the last class of the day and we hope that you all enjoyed the activities we had for you. Now it's time for us to think about the time capsule once again and what we learned from our experience today. Does anyone want to start off sharing some thoughts?"

Alex raised her hand. "I think that things were much different back in 1966."

"How is that, Alex?" Mr. Federici asked.

Alex shrugged her shoulders. "Well, things seemed a lot more simple back then. For example, nobody had cell phones or I-pods to play music with."

Mrs. Bowden nodded her head. "Excellent point, Alex. And that just goes to show us how much technology has evolved over the past forty years. Tell us what kinds of things they did have back in 1966 that we also have today."

Sean H. raised his hand. "They had color TV's by that time, but they were not as nice as the ones we have today. For example, they didn't have big flat screen TV's that you could put on your wall. They were much smaller."

"Great point, Sean," Mr. Federici declared. "And, what's another thing we can say about television sets back in 1966? They didn't have something that we have come to rely on today quite a bit."

Andre J. Garant

"My grandmother has an old TV that still has rabbit ears on it," Stefan pointed out.

"Okay, good example, Stefan, but what did the TV's back then *not* have that we have on TV's today?" Mrs. Buyak asked.

Billy practically jumped out of his seat. "I know, would it be WWE live movies?" Everyone started laughing.

"Nice try, Billy, and you're right, but not exactly the answer I was looking for," Mrs. Buyak commented as she grinned at the fourth grader who slunk back down in his seat with a sheepish grin.

Cassidy was confident that she knew the answer. "I think it would have to be remote controls. They had no such thing back in 1966."

"Perfect answer," Mrs. Bowden called out. "And that is exactly right. In the olden days, people actually had to get up and change the channel using a dial on the television. What else did the TV's back in 1966 not have that we have today?"

Brandon raised his hand. "I'm going to take a guess on this one, but would it be cable or satellite?"

Mr. Federici clapped his hands together. "Perfect answer, Brandon, and that is exactly correct. In the olden days, TV sets only had a few channels and you had to get them using the rabbit ear antennas that Stefan just mentioned. When the reception was bad, the channel was all snowy. You may have seen this when the cable goes out on your own TV set at home."

"I think another thing that is true about TV's in the olden days is that they were a lot smaller,"

Splat!

CJ stated. "You had to sit right up close to them in order to see the picture."

"All great points, everyone," Mrs. Buyak declared. "Let's think about technology a little bit more. How has it evolved since 1966 aside from the television set? Think about something we use every day here in school."

"I'm going to guess it has to do with computers," Eric remarked. "I don't think they had them back in 1966."

"Excellent observation, Eric," Mr. Federici said. "I think the first computers were used back in the 1970's, and even those were extremely obsolete. It really wasn't until the early 1980's that computers were becoming popular as a household item, and they weren't used much in schools until around 1990."

Andy raised his hand. "Mr. Federici, what year was it that the internet was invented?"

"Wow, great question, Andy," Mr. Federici exclaimed. "I'm really happy to see that all of you have your thinking caps on today. The internet was founded back in the early 1990's and started to become popular around 1994. By 2000, I believe that a third of the US population had the internet in their home."

"These are great observations," Mrs. Bowden called out. "Does anyone know how people used to access the internet when it first came out?"

"With a computer," Ethan blurted out, knowing the answer at once.

Mrs. Bowden shook her head. "That's not what I meant, Ethan. Nowadays people access the internet with a high speed cable connection, but how was it done when the internet first came out?"

"I know the answer," Hannah exclaimed. "Was it done with a phone?"

"That is partially correct, Hannah," Mrs. Buyak answered. "It was done not through a phone itself, but through a phone line that was called a dial-up connection. You had to actually dial in like a phone does and you could get disconnected whenever the phone line cut off."

"Isn't that kind of the way a fax works?" Jake asked, not sounding too sure of himself.

"Wow, that was a great observation, Jake," Mr. Federici commented. "Excellent point. A fax runs on a phone line which is why you can hear it dial up and connect. That is exactly how the internet used to work at first, but now most everyone uses a high speed cable connection that is always connected. There is no more dial up connection."

"Since we're on the subject of phones right now, who can tell us the main difference between phones back in 1966 and the phones we use today?" Mrs. Bowden asked.

A bunch of hands went up at once, but Aaron was the first person to be called on. "I believe that the old phones had a twisty wire on them. You couldn't just walk all over the house with them."

"Yeah, I think that phones today are called wireless phones," Jenny pointed out.

"Great job, kids," Mr. Federici explained. "In our homes today, nearly all phones are what we call wireless or remote phones and work the same way that cell phones do. But, that's not the only difference between phones back in 1966 and the

Splat!

phones we use today. Does anyone know what I'm referring to?"

It took a few seconds before some hands went up. Madison was chosen to speak. "I know that my great grandmother is still alive and she has a very old phone that has a circular dial on the front and that is how she dials the number. Her phone doesn't have the buttons that the phones we use in our house have."

"Excellent, Madison," Mrs. Buyak declared. "When phones first came out way back in the real olden days, they were even more primitive. But back in the 1960's and 1970's, most phones had a rotary dial on the front. Once the 1980's came around, the phones converted to have push buttons on the front."

"This is such great information," Noah declared, seeming to be genuinely interested in the topic at hand. "I think I might want to become a historian when I grow up."

Mr. Federici nodded his head. "That would be great, Noah. Keep in mind that you can also become a teacher of history for high school students. The world is changing so quickly today that it would be a great thing to study so that students in modern times know how the world operated in the earlier days."

"We're focusing on technology right now, but there are many other things we could discuss that were different back in 1966," Mrs. Bowden explained. "But, before we move on, who else wants to ask a question or make a point about how technology has evolved?"

"What about cell phones?" Stephon asked. "When did they get invented?"

Andre J. Garant

"Great question, Stephon," Mrs. Buyak remarked. "I can say that cell phones were invented back in the 1980's, but most people didn't have one until the mid 1990's. In fact, I got my first cell phone back in 1997 and it was a very large device that was hard to fit in any pocket. I had to carry it in my pocketbook."

"Exactly right, kids," Mr. Federici continued. "Cell phones are now so advanced that you can fit them right in your pocket and you can also text on them. Texting was not widely known until just a few years ago."

"Kids, what other modern device do we use today that was not used back in 1966?" Mrs. Bowden asked us. "Think about the things we use today to remember certain events."

"Would it be a digital camera?" Zola asked.

"That's exactly right, Zola," Mr. Federici remarked. "Digital cameras are so advanced today and they come in all shapes, colors and sizes. I didn't get my first digital camera until 2003. What kinds of cameras did we use before digital cameras and how were they used?"

Justin raised his hand. "My grandfather likes to take pictures and still uses a camera that has film inside of it. He has to process the film in a darkroom where he makes the pictures."

"Perfect answer, Justin," Mrs. Buyak stated. "The old camera used film to make the pictures and if the film was exposed to light, it was ruined. Can anyone think of a major difference between a film camera and a digital camera aside from how the pictures are made?"

Jack was the first to raise his hand. "Was it megapixels?"

Splat!

Mrs. Bowden shook her head. "Not exactly what I was thinking of, but that's a very good guess, Jack."

Griffin's hand shot up in the air. "I think it has to do with how many pictures you can take. My parents have a digital camera and they take hundreds of pictures of me whenever we go on vacation. They say the camera can hold over a thousand pictures."

"Exactly right, Griffin," Mr. Federici pointed out. "Digital cameras are so advanced today that a tiny little card goes inside of it and can store thousands of pictures without having to delete any. The major difference in a digital camera versus a film camera is that you can see the pictures as you take them. If you recall, a digital camera has a little screen on it that shows the picture. Film cameras didn't have this. The main advantage is that you can see the pictures as you are taking them, and if you don't like them, you can delete the picture right away."

"So, with a film camera you had no idea how the picture would look until you developed the film in a darkroom?" Jason asked.

"That's exactly right, Jason," Mrs. Buyak commented. "And, it could take a week or more before you would get your pictures back to see what they looked like. With most film cameras, you would either send the film out in the mail or bring it to a drug store like Walgreens for processing, and it could take a long time before you ever saw the pictures."

"Does that mean that old film cameras are no longer used now?" Melody asked.

Andre J. Garant

"Yeah, are they considered antiques?" Zach inquired.

Mrs. Bowden wasn't quite sure of the answer. "I don't know if film cameras are antiques since some people still use them, but they will definitely become obsolete at some point in time."

Erin raised her hand. "If my grandfather has a very old camera that he bought about thirty years ago, would it be worth a lot of money today?"

Mr. Federici nodded his head. "That is possible, Erin, but the answer would have to come from an antique appraiser. They could look at the camera and determine if it is worth some money. There are many things to consider, like what shape the camera is in, how old it is, what make it is, and so on."

"This is really neat stuff," Dakota exclaimed. "I really think I'd like to work in a museum someday and study things from the past."

Mrs. Bowden was impressed. "I'm glad you feel that way, Dakota. Let's talk for a few minutes about food. Can you tell me what things you noticed from 1966?"

"They didn't have devil dogs back then?" Anthony blurted out.

Mrs. Bowden laughed. "Tell me something else, Anthony. Let's think about cereal for a minute. When you take a walk down the cereal aisle in your favorite grocery store today, what kinds of things do you notice?"

"Well, I go straight for the Boo Berry and Count Chocula," Donny pointed out.

Everyone laughed, but Mrs. Buyak made the peace signal with her hand. "And that's exactly a

Splat!

good point, Donny. How many types of cereal are there today for kids in fourth grade?"

"A lot," Garrett shouted.

Grace raised her hand to remind her classmates of the proper way to answer a question. "I would say there are at least thirty or forty kinds of cereal for kids today and they all have a lot of sugar in them since that is what kids like to eat."

"Perfect answer, Grace," Mrs. Bowden called out. "Kids love sugar, and so today is a much better era for kids to grow up in than it was in 1966 if you like sweet cereals."

Camille was quick to agree. "Yeah, that Product 19 stuff was just plain yucky looking."

"But a kid growing up in 1966 had that orangey tang stuff to drink," Adrian pointed out. "That stuff looked pretty yummy to me."

Mr. Federici raised his hand to quiet the fourth grade crowd. "That is very true, Adrian, but today there are literally tons of things for kids to drink that did not exist in 1966. For one, there are literally a dozen different type of juices on the market today, many more choices for soda, and you also have different flavors of milk, like chocolate, strawberry, and vanilla."

Brianna D. raised her hand. "I think today is a much better time for kids to grow up in. I say that because of all the advances we have in food and drinks, and also in technology. We can listen to I-pods, work on computers, and watch big TV's that have remote control on them."

"You hit the nail on the head, Brianna," Mrs. Buyak remarked. "And that is a great way to sum up our conversation on the differences between 1966 and today, everyone. There is one final point

Andre J. Garant

I want to make about what has developed along with the internet. That has to do with research and how a typical fourth grader could go about researching a topic to do a homework assignment on it."

"What do you mean?" Mandy asked. "Wouldn't you just a read a book on it?"

"Exactly my point, Mandy," Mrs. Buyak continued. "Back in 1966, a typical fourth grader who wanted to write a book report on Benjamin Franklin would have to go to the local library and read books on him. How would it be done today?"

Jacob S. raised his hand. "By using the internet."

Mr. Federici clapped his hands to signal that Jacob was right on the money. "And that is the main difference between fourth graders today and back in 1966. You don't even have to leave your house today in order to research a topic. You can surf the internet right on the computer in your room using a high speed internet connection. Modern technology has made our lives so much easier today to get any kind of information."

"And we can even use our digital cameras to take pictures of stuff and put that in our report on Benjamin Franklin, like if we went to a museum on him," Jonathan added.

Mrs. Bowden was quick to summarize the events we had discussed. "Boys and girls, when you go home this afternoon, I want all of you to think about what you have learned today. Think about how the life of a typical fourth grader was so different back in 1966. Think about all of the things you have in your home today that make

Splat!

your life so different, whether it be for better or for worse."

"And that brings us to a homework assignment for all of you," Mrs. Buyak explained. "You are to write an essay of at least five hundred words on how your life would be more complicated if you were a fourth grader back in 1966. Your essay is due next Tuesday. Explain why your life would be harder to live and be more complicated in general."

"Aww, man, I thought we were through with homework for this year," John complained.

"Not even close, my friend," Mrs. Bowden commented as she patted the boy on the head.

I then walked over to my teacher and told him how I felt. "You know, Mr. Federici, I think today was a really great day. Not only did I have a great time with all of my classmates doing a bunch of different activities, but I really learned how lucky I am to be growing up in 2011 and not 1966."

My teacher smiled at me. "That's great, Joey, and now you should have an easy time on your essay if you just put that down in words."

I then glanced around the classroom at all of my friends and thought about how great life was for us. Sure, our parents and teachers might yell at us once in a while, but we had so many great things to be thankful for, like color TV's, I-pods, digital cameras, computers, cell phones, and so on. I couldn't imagine a better life to live, and especially when I went to such a great school like that of Eli Terry in South Windsor, Connecticut. Yeah, life sure was good for a ten-year-old boy growing up in 2011!